INCOGNITO

THE LUCIE RIZZO MYSTERY SERIES

ADRIENNE GIORDANO

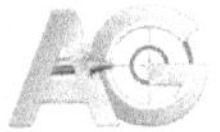

JUSTIFIABLE CAUSE SERIES

The Chase

The Evasion

The Capture

CASINO FORTUNA SERIES

Deadly Odds

JUSTICE SERIES w/MISTY EVANS

Stealing Justice

Cheating Justice

Holiday Justice

Exposing Justice

Undercover Justice

Protecting Justice

Missing Justice

Defending Justice

STEELE RIDGE SERIES w/KELSEY BROWNING

& TRACEY DEVLYN

Steele Ridge: The Beginning

Going Hard (Kelsey Browning)

Living Fast (Adrienne Giordano)

Loving Deep (Tracey Devlyn)

Breaking Free (Adrienne Giordano)

Roaming Wild (Tracey Devlyn)

Stripping Bare (Kelsey Browning)

Enduring Love

STEELE RIDGE: THE KINGSTONS

Craving Heat (Adrienne Giordano)

Tasting Fire (Kelsey Browning)

Searing Need (Tracey Devlyn)

Striking Edge (Coming Soon)

Burning Ache (Coming Soon)

Incognito: A Lucie Rizzo Mystery
Copyright © 2019 by Adrienne Giordano
ISBN: 978-1-942504-29-0
Cover Art by Lewellen Designs
Editing by Gina Bernal and Elizabeth Neal

INCOGNITO

THE LUCIE RIZZO MYSTERY SERIES

ADRIENNE GIORDANO

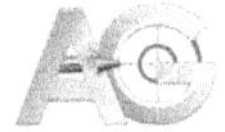

ONE

"Get out."

Lucie glanced up from the report she'd just shoved into her to-do folder. A very large one that sat on top of all the others she'd prepared for Roseanne.

Across from her, Ro sat at her desk in the Coco Barknell headquarters, a long, red-tipped finger spearing the air. With the way she jabbed that finger, Lucie's BFF meant business.

Lucie set her hand on the stack of reports, to-do lists, and schedule changes. "Listen, smart mouth, by tomorrow morning you'll be thanking me. This is everything you'll need while I'm gone."

Rising from her chair, Ro cornered the desk, her three-pounds-lighter hips swinging as she double-timed it to Lucie. She held out a hand and pointed to the door with the other. "Give me those. And get out."

Lucie glanced at Tim—O'Hottie as Ro called him—her Chicago PD detective boyfriend of six months. In that time, Lucie had learned a lot about Tim O'Brien, and that tight-lipped, I'm-about-to-lose-my-shit look he'd pinned on her didn't bode well for the start of their vacation. One that included visiting his favorite uncle near Palm Beach for a few days before going to the Keys. For weeks he'd been heading off any possible issues that would impede their trip.

Now, with her stalling, O'Hottie might finally be hitting the upper boundary of his patience. With Tim, that was saying something. The man was destined for sainthood, no doubt.

Still, she didn't want to start their trip off with an argument. Not after they'd sprung for the mighty expensive first-class upgrade. "I'm almost ready," she said.

"Luce, please. Our flight is in ninety minutes. And it's rush hour."

"Swear to God," Ro said, "If you don't get out, I'll kill you where you stand." She yanked Lucie's hand from the stack of reports and shoved her, literally, to the door. "Go. We're all adults. The business won't collapse because you're on vacation. And, you know, there's this terrific invention called a telephone. If we need you, we'll call." She swung the office door open and did a little toodles wave. "Buh-bye now."

When Lucie didn't move, Ro clasped her elbow and squeezed. Hard.

"Ow. You don't have to get nasty."

"Sister, you've worked your ass off building this company and finally have enough backup to take a well-deserved vacation. I promise you, we've got this. I'll cover the phones and client calls. Joey will handle the dog-walking side. We're all good. Please. Trust me."

Of course she did. They'd been friends since grammar school. If there was anyone she trusted with her business, it was Ro.

But this wasn't about that. This was about control and giving it up.

They stopped at the door and Lucie turned back to Tim. The overhead light reflected off red hair that, in days, would slip to strawberry blond under the sun's rays. With his fair skin, he'd need a gallon or twelve of sunscreen. He scooped up her suitcase and carry-on, his yummy muscles handling them with ease. "They've got it, Luce. They'll call if they need you. Now, please get your cute little ass moving before we miss this flight. That'd definitely piss me off."

Everyone wanted her out. After everything she'd put into growing Coco Barknell, none of them could understand what it took to leave. Sure, Ro had been there from the beginning, helping Lucie expand her one dog-walking client to a pet care and handmade accessories company. Want an animal print vest for your poodle? Coco Barknell provided it. Plus sizes too.

In the last year, they'd gone from Lucie running things on her own to employing three full-timers and two part-time dog walkers. And for the first time, Lucie was turning over the reins.

A lot could happen in ten days. Total annihilation, for example.

"Girlfriend," Ro said, waving her hand to encompass the room, "I know this is killing you, but I promise I'll take care of everything. I've always got your back."

She looked back at Ro, who'd kicked the crap out of Tiffy Nelson in the third grade and showed that bully why she should never, *ever* pick on Lucie. Through twenty years of friendship they'd shared first loves, heartbreaks, and Lucie's conflicted feelings about the notoriety that came with being mob boss Joe Rizzo's kid.

The mob princess.

That was Lucie. Even her Notre Dame education couldn't free her from that moniker.

"It's just..." Lucie spun back to Tim, who grunted at her. Lord, if she didn't get moving, he'd lose it. This wasn't fair. He worked insane hours, constantly receiving calls from his lieutenant and barely getting two full days off every week. Now he had ten and she was stressing him out. Lucie held both hands up. "Okay. Okay. I'm sorry."

Ro shoved her out the door. "Go. Before O'Hottie loses his Irish temper. As much fun as *that* would be, it's a heck of a way to start a vacation. Besides, what could go wrong?"

Oh, she didn't just say that. Lucie whirled back.

"Shit," Tim said.

Lucie flapped her arms and let out the mother of all sighs. "Let's face it, things haven't exactly been calm around here."

"I'm done." He nudged her rear with her suitcase. "Move it. Before I wind up going alone. Roseanne, thank you. Even though I could strangle you right now."

"Eh," Ro said, "story of my life. Get out."

The crowd at the baggage carousel had thinned to one lone airline employee lining up yet-to-be-claimed luggage. Lucie's suitcase had gone the wrong direction. The way wrong direction.

"It's a sign," she said as they left the customer service counter, claim ticket in hand.

"It's *not* a sign. It's two hundred people on a plane with a ton of luggage. We were late and yours just didn't make it. It happens."

That was her fault? Maybe she'd delayed them leaving the office, but she didn't control Chicago traffic. "Yours made it."

He halted in front of the now motionless carousel and

peered down at her, his green eyes gentle, as always. But she knew him. His mind was moving at warp speed, searching for a comeback. It took a solid ten seconds before he shook his head and a reluctant smile tugged at his lips. "I can't argue with you. Ever. You're too damned cute."

"It's a gift."

"Don't I know it." He popped a light kiss on her mouth. "It's one of the many things I love about you. Don't worry. They said you'd have it by morning. We'll buy a toothbrush and you can sleep in one of my T-shirts." He waggled his eyebrows. "I always enjoy that."

"Timothy Aloysius!"

Tim angled back to where a man wearing a Hawaiian-print shirt and khaki shorts waved. His full—and shocking—head of white hair against the deep brown skin on his trim build worked with the whole Florida vacation vibe. Despite the hair, from a distance he appeared to be in his late fifties. This had to be Tim's Uncle Henry.

And, hello? Tim's middle name was Aloysius? She squeezed his hand, more than ready to capitalize on this surprise. "How did I not know that?"

"I guess you're still learning."

"I guess so. Sounds like a monk's name. But we sure know you're not one."

Not with his libido. He met her eye and a zing of heat sparked between them. Tim liked sex. A lot. In the two weeks leading up to this trip he'd offered suggestions regarding the frequency in which he'd like to have said sex. Which was pretty much constantly.

The man worked hard. He deserved it. Lucie would— cough, cough—*suffer* through it.

Tim brought his attention back to his uncle. "Hey, Uncle Henry." He let go of his suitcase and they embraced in the manly, backslapping way that should've knocked loose a few organs.

"My God." Uncle Henry pulled back. "You gained weight. Look at you. You're like a linebacker now."

Between Lucie's mom shoving homemade desserts at him every time he stepped through the door and his brother's restaurant, Tim's once lanky frame had filled out in the past year. Twenty-five pounds worth that kept him on a relentless workout schedule to keep from turning doughy.

"Vast amounts of good food do that." Tim slid his arm over Lucie's shoulder. "This one is part of the problem. Why didn't anyone warn me not to fall in love with an Italian girl?"

Aww, how sweet was that? Gosh, she knew how to pick a good man.

She tipped her head sideways, leaning into Tim and not bothering to fight the happy grin lighting her up. "Hello, Mr. Brennan. I've heard a lot about you."

Lucie held her hand out, but Tim's uncle swatted it away, opening his arms to her instead. "Forget that formal stuff. I come from a long line of huggers. And call me Henry. Or Uncle Henry. Whatever."

Henry's arms came around her and crunched a rib or two on her 110-pound frame. A burst of air shot from her mouth. Holy smokes, her eyes may have popped out. For such a lean man, Uncle Henry packed some strength.

"It's good to finally meet you, Lucie. My nephew speaks highly of you." He released her and pointed at Tim's suitcase. "Is that everything?"

"For now. Lucie's bag wound up in North Dakota. They'll deliver it tomorrow."

"Ach. I'm sorry. I have extra toothbrushes and soap at the house."

Henry led them to the parking lot and his Lexus. According to Tim's mom, pre-retirement Uncle Henry worked for a once small airline that grew—and grew—over the twenty-seven years of his employment. From the start, he'd bought stock through a discounted employee purchase plan that allowed him to make a killing when the company went public.

And gave him the means to retire at fifty-five.

Thus, the home in Paradise City, a cushy, self-contained forty-five square mile community in Palm Beach County. Two hundred thousand folks over the age of fifty enjoyed, as the website said, an active lifestyle. Golf courses, beaches, restaurants, a square with retail shops and several top of the line gyms, plus, a clubhouse complete with commercial kitchen were just a few of the amenities. Lucie's favorite was the transportation of choice. A golf cart.

While the men loaded the luggage, Lucie climbed into the back seat. Tim had long legs and needed more room.

"I see you still have the Lexus," Tim said.

"Sure. It's ten years old and has thirty-thousand miles. Why sell it? Besides, I take the cart most places."

Lucie suddenly had a vision of Roseanne tooling around Franklin in a golf cart. For some odd reason, it fit.

Uncle Henry paid the parking attendant and cruised through the gate. "Did you two eat? We can stop somewhere."

"We're good," Tim said. "We splurged on first class. It's also nine-thirty. Way past your bedtime."

Uncle Henry laughed and something inside Lucie bloomed. Seeing Tim with his family, experiencing the fierce love they shared, did that to her.

"I know, young man," Henry said. "I had to drink an extra cup before leaving to pick you up. My Matilda makes great coffee." Henry met Lucie's eye in the rearview mirror. "Lucie, do you like coffee? My Matilda makes excellent coffee."

His Matilda. How cute was he?

"Finally," Tim said. "I'll get to sample it. I'm damned tired of hearing how good it is."

Being a mainliner, Tim could be a harsh critic. Lucie? Coffee was coffee. She didn't consider herself a connoisseur. She just needed a good hit of caffeine every now and again.

Tim angled sideways, facing Henry. "Full disclosure. Mom gave me strict orders to check this woman out. She doesn't want some ho getting her hooks into her little brother."

Oh, he did *not* just call his uncle's girlfriend that. "Tim!"

"What's a ho?" Henry asked.

Lucie burst out laughing. Poor Henry. Or maybe poor Tim since he was making a joke at his uncle's expense and it wound up a wasted effort. When Tim didn't respond, Uncle Henry met Lucie's gaze in the mirror again. "Lucie, what's a ho?"

"Well, sir, simply put, a slut." Silence ensued. At least until both men snorted.

"My sister," Henry said. "She's too much."

"She worries about you."

"I'm fifty-eight years old and I'm alone. Doesn't she want me happy?"

"Hell yeah, she does. But you know her. She's protective."

With Tim's mad protective instincts, that apple didn't fall from the tree. According to Tim, Henry's wife passed away two years earlier after a short stint with an aggressive cancer. They'd been married thirty-five years and the loss had devastated Henry. Which prompted the move to Florida for a fresh start. Now, Matilda had shown up, Henry was googly-eyed, and Tim's mother didn't trust it.

Not for one second.

Henry removed one hand from the steering wheel and poked a finger in the air. "She's never met Mattie. Not even a phone conversation. How would she know anything about our relationship? She's kind and beautiful. Everyone loves her. You'll see. She cooks for me, makes sure I take my blood pressure pills, checks on me all day. She gives me a foot rub every night."

Tim swiveled back to Lucie. "Foot rub. Every night. You taking notes?"

"Oh, I am," she said. "That goes both ways, O'Hottie. If you're getting one, so am I."

"Deal," he said.

"Deal."

And if she knew Tim at all, even an iota, she knew it'd come with plenty of innuendos and foreplay that would land them right in bed. Which might be great for Tim's libido, but Lucie? She'd need a lot of naps if she intended on keeping up with the sexual marathon.

Clearly happy with their bargain, Tim turned to face the front again. "When do we get to meet Mattie?"

"Tomorrow night. It's Tiki Night at the beach club. We can walk or take the cart. Usually I walk. I don't like to drink and drive. Three months ago, Benny Stuart drove home loaded and didn't see his neighbor walking her dog. Plowed right into her."

Tim choked out a half-laugh. "No way."

"Don't laugh, son. The woman broke her hip and Benny is doing community service. If that wasn't enough, now there's a civil suit and the homeowners association banned driving golf carts while intoxicated."

As if it shouldn't have been before? Nothing like a group of plastered senior citizens tearing it up in golf carts. Thank goodness her parents didn't live here. The idea of her father driving one around and screaming at people to get the hell out of the way made her shudder.

"Wow," Lucie said. "Who knew?"

After flipping his blinker on, Henry made a smooth turn on Paradise Way where a large brick sign welcomed visitors.

"It's causing a ruckus," Henry said. "The association is trying to mandate seat belts in the carts. Do you know what that would cost?"

"Well, Unc, grading on a curve, it'll be cheaper than getting sued. A permanent injury to someone could be a million-dollar lawsuit. Maybe more. I'd consider it."

Oh, the problems of retirees. Lucie refrained from shaking her head. Uncle Henry and her father's lives were so different. Henry's biggest concern was his sister not liking his girlfriend and driving a cart sober. Her dad? He'd just gotten out of jail on a two-year tax evasion charge that was the government's only shot at incarcerating a notorious mob boss. At any time, Lucie fully expected the Feds to come knocking on the Rizzo front door.

Henry waved a hand. "Anyway, don't get me riled up. What were we talking about?"

"Mattie," Lucie said.

"Ah, yes. My sweet Mattie. Tomorrow night you'll meet her."

"Tiki Night," Tim said. "Can't wait."

Even in the dark, Lucie spotted the stink-eye Henry threw Tim's way. "Don't knock it until you try it. Live music and a buffet for nineteen ninety-five. Cash bar though. We're trying to get them to include the bar in the price. Cheap bastards."

Tim glanced back at Lucie. "What do you think? Tiki Night tomorrow?"

"Did I mention the club is right on the beach?"

Hmmm...hanging out with a bunch of retirees or a quiet night with Tim? As much as she wanted time alone with her man, the people watching would be amazing.

She smiled wide. "I wouldn't miss it."

TWO

The next afternoon at T-minus one hour to Tiki Night, Lucie took her handsome Irish detective up on an offer of a walk on the beach. The festivities started at four and Henry didn't want them dawdling, but after spending the day exploring the area with Tim and his uncle, she needed downtime.

As promised, her suitcase arrived by eight that morning and she'd organized her outfits for the next few days. Now freshly showered, she slipped into her flip flops and checked the full-length mirror mounted on the back of the bedroom door. She'd dressed in long white denim shorts to cover her spindly, I-need-some-sun legs. Paired with them was a tank top that showed a hint of cleavage she knew would drive Tim insane.

Heh, heh, heh.

Despite her petite size, Mother Nature blessed her with a healthy set of boobs that caused Tim to go mad.

Call it relationship security, because when she flashed it, the man was toast. Total goner.

She'd also taken a few extra minutes to put on a light layer of makeup. Unlike Ro, Lucie didn't opt for the sexy vixen look. It didn't work for her. Once in a while, when heading out for a special evening, yes, she went for it. On the daily? Nah. It wasn't her and Tim didn't care for it.

For tonight, she'd gone the extra distance and straightened her hair. The moist, ocean air would kink it up a bit, but half a can of hairspray might help.

All in all, Miss Completely Average wasn't so average anymore.

"Luce," Tim called from beyond the bedroom door, "losing daylight here. Henry'll be irritated if we don't show up at four o'clock sharp."

Losing daylight in the middle of the afternoon? Lucie snorted.

Satisfied with her appearance, she whipped open the door. "Coming, Detective."

She strode into the living room where Tim sat in Henry's recliner flipping through channels on the wall-mounted television. He turned his head and—yep—his gaze torpedoed straight to her cleavage.

Did she know this man or what?

He let out a low whistle that sent a shot of heat to her core. "Hopefully, that means it was worth the wait."

"You always are." He popped out of the chair, walked to her, and cupped her cheeks in his big hands. "Vacation looks good on you."

Then he kissed her. Nothing too crazy in Uncle Henry's living room because who even knew where he might be, but enough that the soft touch of lips let her know there'd be more—a lot more—later.

Vacation. *Yay, Lucie.*

He pulled back and she smiled up at him. "Losing daylight here."

Tim gave her the classic O'Brien smile his siblings had all seemed to master. The one that was half sarcasm and half genuine amusement. "You're a wicked woman, Luce."

They strolled the three blocks toward the club where a grass hut had been placed on the boardwalk in front of a two-story pale pink building with white arched windows. Everything about the place said Florida, wealth, and comfort.

"Nice place," Lucie said.

"Uncle Henry says it's the hot spot. Beach club and restaurant by day, club by night."

"Fun. Honestly, if the idea of my father harassing people in golf carts didn't terrify me, I'd say my parents should look into a place like this."

"Luce come on. Joe Rizzo at Paradise City? They wouldn't exactly blend."

"I disagree. Down here, no one would know them. Total anonymity. Unless, of course, there's a large Chicago contingency. I'd have to look into that." She held up a finger. "I'll ask Henry. This would be good for my folks."

At the edge of the boardwalk, Tim kicked off the leather slides Lucie bought for him and scooped them up. He despised the feeling of sand in his shoes. Another thing she'd learned about him. Following suit, Lucie kicked off her flip flops while glancing at the breaking waves. She inhaled salty moist air. Her dad loved the water. Any kind. Rivers, lakes, oceans. All of it.

"Your dad will never leave Chicago."

"How do you know?"

Tim shrugged. "He told me."

Lucie stopped walking. Her father, notoriety aside, kept

his private life on the downlow. He never shared details about his kids or wife. In fact, he rarely commented on anything Joe Rizzo. He'd sling his line of bull and deflect questions.

Over the years, Lucie had adjusted to the idea that he kept his business and personal life separate. Something she never minded because, really, she didn't approve of his lifestyle. No girl wanted to hear about her father's illegal exploits.

Where he intended to live permanently? She'd have appreciated hearing that from him. Instead, he'd shared it with Tim. Had to be a reason. Dad never did anything without a purpose.

She pushed the hurt from her heart. "He *told* you that?"

"Yeah. That night you were late for dinner, your dad and I were talking. He asked about my folks. I told him they were looking to be snowbirds and he said he'd never leave Chicago. His life is there. And his kids. He won't leave you and Joey. His stint in jail and the lost time when you guys were little were enough."

Lucie shook her head. "Wow. Are you sure it was my dad?"

Tim slipped his hand through hers and squeezed. "There's only one Joe. Thank God. I think he regrets not being there for you two. Definitely your mom."

"Even when he wasn't in jail, he wasn't around a lot. His crew was more important."

"That's too bad."

She shrugged. "We got used to it."

"Anyway," Tim said, "he seemed pretty set on staying in Chicago." He tipped his head to the sky, taking in the warm afternoon sun. "I wonder if he's ever been to Florida in March. It beats the hell out of snow and slush."

Lucie's feet sunk into the sand as she walked, reminding her that she couldn't agree more. "It sure does."

"What about you, Luce? Would you ever leave?"

At this point, she had her business and family, but if she had to, yes, she would. "I guess if the opportunity was right, I could."

"You didn't when Frankie asked you."

Frankie. A subject she and Tim didn't broach all that often. Tim knew Frankie had been her first love, and no man wanted to compete with that. He'd done the only thing he could and made it easy for her to love him for all the things Frankie wasn't.

After years of begging Frankie to leave their hometown and their mob kid reputations behind, he'd decided to move to New York. After they'd broken up. That alone seemed like a betrayal. Then he'd shown up and asked her to move with him, knowing she'd just started the business. She'd informed Tim of all of it.

As much as she'd tried to convince him Frankie was history, Tim had insecurities. She clasped his hand harder as they strolled the beach.

"I suppose the right guy hasn't asked me."

"Huh. So, if the right guy did, you'd do it? Self-sufficient, Lucie Rizzo would pick up her life and go? For a man?" This time, Tim stopped walking and faced her. "Luce, if *I* asked, would you do it?"

"Are you?"

"No. Well, not yet. I'm thirty-five years old, Luce, and I want kids. I plan on retiring by the time I'm fifty and this warm weather might not be a bad idea. Kids need to go to school—or be homeschooled, but I don't see myself as the homeschool type. Being a snowbird won't work for me until they're out of high school. If I intend to spend winters in a more moderate climate, I'd have to move out of Illinois."

"You'd leave your family?"

He shrugged. "It's not like I'd never see them again. My folks are looking to be snowbirds, at a minimum."

Was he asking her to move with him? Have kids? Could she do that without some sort of commitment? Marriage? She liked to think of herself as progressive, but, down deep, she wanted to be married before having children.

"Hmm," she said. "You threw me a little with this conversation."

"You know I love you."

Yes. She absolutely knew that. "I do. I love you too. In ways I never thought possible. You accept me and my crazy family without judgment. For that alone, I'll love you forever."

"But you're not answering my question. Is leaving Chicago a deal breaker?"

No. But she did have a business to run. "I don't think so."

Tim let out a sigh. "That wasn't exactly what I was hoping for."

"Hey, you surprised me. I wasn't prepared is all." She circled a hand around her head. "You know me, I have to process. I have a business there. Ro could probably run it, if she wanted. Maybe we could expand. Open another office in the south. There are all sorts of possibilities, so nothing is out of the question. In terms of the company."

"Uh-oh. Why do I feel like there's a but?"

"Because there is. Once you retire from law enforcement, you'll have the freedom to do whatever you want. I'm a business owner. Unless I sell, I'll never have that. I will always have responsibilities. I also want a family. I want to be married. Have a couple kids." She turned and faced him. "I want my fairy tale. If I move, I'd expect you to give me that."

Ugh. Talk about giving a man an ultimatum. Marry me or else.

His mouth dropped open. "That's what you're worried about? Me proposing?"

When he said it like that, it sounded silly, as if she was some dimwitted, high schooler conjuring her perfect life. "Not exactly *that*, but, you know, a...commitment. Of some sort."

"Lucie, if I didn't think both our families would freak, I'd marry you tomorrow. Fly to Vegas and get it done."

Oh, good answer. "Really?"

"*Pfft. I've* been giving *you* space. I figured if we got to a year of seeing each other, I'd bring it up. We've only been together six months."

"Technically, it's six and three quarters."

He laughed. "Whatever. But since we're getting clear on what we want, if I asked you to marry me and have a bunch of redheaded O'Brien babies—"

A bunch? Grandma Rizzo, an inch shorter than her, may have popped out six babies, but Lucie? No way. She stared down at her crotch as if it would suddenly wave a white flag. "Hang on, Detective. I didn't say a *bunch*. I said a couple. Maybe, if my vagina doesn't shred, I'd go to three. *Maybe*."

"Yada, yada," Tim said. "It's a negotiating point for a later date. We're establishing framework here."

She gave him an eye roll. Were they really doing this? The little flutter in her belly sure thought so. "Fine."

"For *framework* purposes, if I asked you to marry me and pop out some kids, you'd be okay leaving Chicago?"

She made a show of tilting her head one way, then the other.

"Luce, seriously? You're breaking my stones *now*?"

"You can't rush a girl." When he shook his head, she squeezed his hand and tried to get to her tiptoes to kiss him, but her feet dug into the sand making her miss her mark. He helped by bending low, so she wrapped her hand over the back of his head and hit him with a smacking kiss. "I love you. And, yes, I'd leave with you. If that's what you need to be happy, and you'll support me in my business, we'll make it work."

RIDING the high of talking about a future filled with a brood of O'Brien babies, Lucie made her way up the beach, her hand wrapped inside Tim's and the sun warming her cheeks. Suddenly, the possibilities in her life seemed endless.

Mrs. Timothy Aloysius O'Brien.

Dad would have a heart attack.

Lucie Rizzo-O'Brien might be better. Still, an Irish last name? That'd be interesting.

Interesting and fun. She grinned up at Tim. When he locked his gaze on hers, that tiny flutter came back. Gosh, she'd gotten lucky. "I like this."

"What?"

"Vacations with you. We're both so busy at home, it's nice to have quiet time and talk."

"It is. We should do this twice a year. Even if it's not the full ten days, maybe we break it up. Do four in the summer and ten in the winter."

Yes. She could wrap her mind around that. When she worked in banking, she always planned her vacations at least a year out to snag the days before any other associates claimed them. Being an entrepreneur didn't allow for a lot of free time. If she had one complaint about running her own business it would be the inability to turn everything off. When self-employed, there was no such thing as a day off. Always emails to tend to, orders to place, checks to write.

Except now. Now she had Tim, a sandy beach, and sunshine. And a future she hadn't even realized she'd been dreaming of.

"You two!"

Uncle Henry stood on the boardwalk waving his arms. Primped and dressed to kill in black cotton shorts and a white button-down, the man looked sharp—relaxed, Florida sharp anyway—and ready for Tiki Night.

"Hey, Unc," Tim called as they closed the last thirty feet.

"It's after four. We gotta get in there before Lois Weinstein grabs the good spot. She's a shady one."

Lucie checked her watch. Four oh three. And Joey made fun of *her* about her obsession with keeping on schedule?

"Sorry," Tim said. "We could have met you inside."

Not bothering to wait, Henry started toward the club entrance, waving them forward. "Let's go."

"Wow," Lucie whispered. "Tiki Night is no joke."

"I guess this is what we have to look forward to in our old age."

Lucie made an ick face. Lord, if her existence ever came down to beating Lois Weinstein to the good seats, she might never retire.

Twenty minutes later, Lucie understood the fuss. Retirees claiming their view of the ocean occupied every available inch of space along the outer deck rails. Henry, bless him, managed to commandeer the only table against the railing and his irritation at their tardiness came full circle.

The good table indeed.

Everywhere Lucie looked she saw gray hair and wrinkly, Florida-baked skin. Talk about bringing down the average age demographic. She and Tim were toddlers compared to them.

"This place is packed," Lucie said.

"That's why we had to get here early. Otherwise, we have to sit back there." He jerked a thumb to the remaining tables situated against the windows. Behind all the crammed-in bodies blocking the view.

"My Mattie, she likes this spot."

Lucie glanced at Tim, who'd managed to smile. His mother had been working him over about getting "intel" on Uncle Henry's girlfriend. All Tim wanted was quality time with his uncle and his mom had given him an assignment. One he wasn't too thrilled with since it put him between his mother, someone he liked to keep happy but wasn't afraid to go against, and his uncle, whom he hadn't seen in years.

This would be the ultimate test of the good detective's mediation skills.

He picked up his beer, took a sip and tilted the end at Henry. "You're really crazy about this woman."

"What's not to be crazy about? She's beautiful and funny. And everyone loves her. You'll see." He circled a finger. "Every man here wants her. I'm beating them off with sticks."

A senior smackdown. How fun would that be? "Sticks, huh?" Lucie leaned over and popped a light kiss on Tim's mouth. "That could be dangerous. Do I need to be worried about Tim falling victim to her charms?"

Tim made a low humming noise that sent Lucie's libido into high gear. Florida. A most excellent place.

"Not a chance," Tim said. "I'm a one-woman man."

"Woohoo," someone cooed. Lucie's mind snapped back to Ro making one of her grand entrances. Please, God, no.

Wait. It couldn't be. First of all, this was Lucie and Tim's vacation, a mere thirteen hundred miles from Chicago. Second, her BFF promised to supervise the business while Lucie took some downtime. And, Ro, being Ro, would never, ever go back on her word. Coco Barknell meant too much to both of them.

"Woohooo!" The voice came again, deeper this time with more of a rasp than Ro's.

Not Ro.

Henry's eyes widened, the glow enough to light an entire room, and he shot from his chair, literally hopping up to see over the crowd.

"Doll." He waved.

Tim's head swiveled sideways, his eyebrows hiking nearly to his hairline. "Doll? My mother would kill herself."

"Ssshhh. He's in love. Leave him alone."

He gave her a soft pat on the thigh. "I'm gonna start calling you doll."

Oh, no. No way. Babe? Fine. Honey? Even better. Doll? She'd skin him. "Not if you want to live, you won't."

He snorted before angling back for his first peep at Uncle Henry's beloved. His relaxed features transformed into the tight lines of his all-business cop face. "Holy crap."

Uh-oh.

Following his lead, she turned. An older woman with deep auburn hair—really *big* auburn hair—and a face full of expertly applied makeup pushed through the crowd, smiling and waving. She squeezed between two couples, and Lucie caught the full brunt of the leopard print top that clung to her boobs, revealing a mountain of cleavage.

No wonder Uncle Henry was beating men off. She

looked like a cross between a high-end madam and a retired stripper.

Poor Tim swung back, his jaw clenched hard enough to crack a few teeth.

"Don't say it," she said.

For a moment, his eyes bugged out. Then his mouth opened and hung there. "I'm...shit. You know what I'm thinking, right?"

She sure did. Strutting toward them in second-skin white leggings and high-heeled sandals was Ro in twenty-five years.

Lucie squeezed his arm. "Just relax. Take a breath or something."

"My mom will stab herself." Tim lifted his hand, jabbed it toward his face. "Right in the eye."

"Stop."

"Holy crap," he repeated as a bead of sweat dripped from him. Lucie handed him a cocktail napkin. *Dab, dab, dab.* He blotted the sweat bubbling on his forehead. "Luce, you have no idea. My aunt, his first wife? She was a saint. I mean, if she wore anything other than a turtleneck, she considered it improper. Covered from head to toe. We used to joke that she was a failed nun."

Before Mattie reached them, she was intercepted. She met Henry's eye for a brief second, the apology evident as a couple pulled her into a brief conversation.

"Mattie!" Another woman called.

All around them, a chorus of "hellos" and "Matties" sounded.

"She's popular," Lucie said.

Uncle Henry peered down at her, a smile still lighting his face. "I told you. Everyone loves her. She's the best."

After a day in the sun, Tim's fair Irish skin had fallen

victim to sunburn, but now the redness faded to a dull green. Between that and the sweating, Lucie put her hand against his cheek. Could he be sick? Maybe the crab cake sandwich at lunch?

"Tim? Are you okay?"

"I'm telling you," he whispered, the words coming in hard punches. "She will stab herself."

Lucie peered up at a smiling Henry. "Well, she might have to adjust."

THREE

Mattie broke free of the crowd and rushed toward Henry, her boobs testing the precarious boundaries of her stretchy shirt.

She reached her arms to Henry and folded him into Camp Cleavage. "Oh, my darling."

Having spent nearly a lifetime with Ro, Lucie recognized a woman's ability to make the most of her assets. Ro usually popped a few extra buttons to make a man fall in line.

Mattie wasn't so subtle.

She pulled back and held Henry's arms. "I'm so sorry to have kept you waiting." She let go of him, swung sideways, and—*whoa*—Lucie couldn't stop staring at her damned boobs. It was like a train derailment. Terrifying, but absorbing at the same time. They were just so…there.

"Hello," Mattie said, holding her arms out. "You must be Tim and Lucie."

When Tim failed to respond—gobsmacked by the rack, no doubt—Lucie slid from her seat to greet the woman.

"Hi, Mattie." She stepped into Boobville, accepting a generous hug topped off with a little squeeze at the end.

Okay. So maybe Mattie was a lot. Maybe a little more than a lot, but she gave great hugs.

Lucie stepped back and spun to Tim. "Say hello to Mattie," she chirped.

When he didn't move, she latched onto his arm and damn near pulled him to his feet.

Come on, man, snap out of it. If it wouldn't make a scene, she'd be tempted to pat his cheek. Knock some life into him.

"Right." He cleared his throat. "Sorry. I was…"

Mattie took a step, obviously intending on laying one of her awesome hugs on him.

He made a strangling noise and Lucie considered running interference but was saved by a woman shoving between them.

"Hello, Mattie," the woman said. "Great crowd tonight. Love your blouse."

"Thank you, Lois. Are we still on for lunch next week?"

Ah. This must be the famous Lois Weinstein, scoping out a spot so she could commandeer the table if they abandoned it.

Not a chance, sister.

"Of course," Lois said to Mattie. "You pick the place."

"Doll," Henry said. "take my seat."

"Thank you, Henry."

Henry slid to the empty chair he'd risked his life saving. "How was your day?"

"Oh, it was fine. You know. Same old thing." She waved at someone, then met Lucie's gaze. "I'm a decorator. Well, not a real one—although, they call them interior designers now. I just help out in the community. I have an eye for these things."

Tim blinked. Had to be the leopard print tripping him up.

"That's wonderful," Lucie said. "My friend, Roseanne, is the same way. Some people just seem to know when something works. I don't have that gift. Ro constantly tells me to stop the madness."

Mattie let out a hoot and patted her hand against her heart, making her left boob jiggle. "I think I'd like this Roseanne."

Mid-gulp of his beer, Tim half-choked, half-gagged and spewed the sudsy brew. Lucie jumped up and smacked his back hard enough to dislodge a lung.

"Are you all right?"

He cleared his throat and held up a hand. "Wrong..." Cough, cough. "Pipe." Cough, cough.

He shook his head, exhaling a heavy breath. Poor guy. In Lucie's nutty family, this wackiness happened on the daily. Tim? His peeps were normal.

At least until Mattie came along and evened things out. *Heh, heh, heh.* Finally, a weakness revealed.

Now, Tim understood, on a much smaller scale, the chaos one over-the-top person could create.

"Oh, my goodness," Mattie said. "You scared me."

Uncle Henry scooted his chair closer to Mattie. "Honey, are you okay?" He set one hand on her forehead, then moved it to her cheek. "Do you feel faint? Need some water?"

Tim's mouth dropped open. Here he was, nearly dying in front of them—well, that may have been an exaggeration, but still—and Henry was worried about Mattie.

Making no bones about it, Tim lifted one hand and pretended to stab himself in the eye.

"Oh." Mattie pressed both hands to Uncle Henry's cheeks. "You are the sweetest man. Always taking care of me." She dropped her hands, straightened her back so her boobs poked out a little more, and glanced at Lucie. "Isn't he the sweetest?"

Lawdy, this woman. A *lot*. Between the big hair, the tight clothes, and the boobs, Lucie wasn't sure where to look. And forget about Tim. He was gone. Completely fried. Lucie set one hand on his leg and squeezed. "Yes. Absolutely the sweetest. Well, next to Tim, of course."

Again Mattie hooted and something about that laugh, the tinkling edge of it that screamed manufactured, put Lucie on alert.

In her lifetime, Lucie had seen a lot of women like Mattie. Ones who needed attention, any attention, from men and grappled for it however they could.

A waitress swung by and Henry ordered another round of drinks for everyone. Including four waters. Just in case Mattie felt faint again.

"Now," Mattie said, "how was everyone's day? Did you enjoy it?"

Lucie nodded. "I know I did. Particularly because it snowed at home today."

"I remember those days. Freezing until June. I don't miss it."

"Where are you from, Mattie?"

"All over really. I lived in the northeast for a while and then headed south." She looked beyond Tim. "There's Eleanor. Eleanor!" She lifted her hand and waved. "Woohoo."

"Hi, Mattie," the woman called back. "I'll see you tomorrow, yes?"

"Looking forward to it. We'll hit that little shop on the boulevard for some lamps."

Mattie came back to them. "I'm sorry about that. Eleanor is one of my clients. I'm working with her tomorrow. Her husband died—God rest his soul—six months ago and she wants to update the house. Give it a fresh look. Out with the old, in with the new."

A pained noise came from somewhere in Tim's throat. All eyes moved to him.

"Sorry." He bumped the side of his fist into his chest. "Still got a little something stuck."

"Ooh, which reminds me." She ran a hand down Henry's arm, stroking gently. "Darling, would you be able to feed and walk Aphrodite tomorrow? You know how she gets if her schedule is interrupted."

Aphrodite?

"You know I will. Anything for you."

While Uncle Henry and Mattie made gag-worthy extended eye contact, Tim leaned over, kissed Lucie's cheek, and whispered. "Forget the eye-stab. My mom will kill herself. Bullet. Right to the head. Bang."

"Thank you, honey," Mattie said. "You're just *so* sweet."

Tim cleared his throat again. "So, Mattie. Aphrodite is your dog?"

"Yes. She's a sweetheart. Henry helps with her when I have to be out of the house for an extended time."

Excellent. A nice, generic topic to explore.

"It's good that you have help," Lucie said. "Dogs can be fussy about their routine. My company provides dog walking and the scheduling is serious business."

"Lucie loves the dogs," Tim said.

"Well, most of them. I do have my favorites I guess."

"Otis," Tim said. "The Ninja Bitches."

Mattie's eyes widened. "The what?"

Lucie laughed. "That's not their real name. They're Shih Tzus. Short on stature and big on attitude. They like Tim, though. They flirted with him the first time they met him."

Lucie thought back to a year ago when a rash of dognappings had plagued her clients. That was the first time she'd met Detective Tim O'Brien. Back then she'd had no idea she'd fall in love with an Irish cop.

Tim ripped off a big smile. "What can I say? I have a way with women."

"How adorable," Mattie cooed.

Lucie had described Tim in many ways over the months.

Alpha.

Patient.

In-charge.

Adorable? Not so much. He'd hate that. Would more than likely rail about it all night.

On cue, he hopped out of his chair. "Excuse me."

Henry eyed him. "Where you going?"

"Restroom," he said.

"Didn't you just go when we walked in?"

Uh-oh.

Lucie jumped in. "He drank a lot of water today. Hydration. It's good for you."

"With my prostate? Please."

Another strangled noise shot from Tim's throat. This must be the cross street between Tim's version of sane and not.

Being accustomed to lunatics, Lucie had no issues holding up the conversation in Tim's absence. "Henry, if you'd like, I'd be happy to help with Aphrodite tomorrow. If Mattie doesn't mind, that is."

"A professional dog walker? I'd never mind that."

"But you're on vacation," Uncle Henry said.

"Yes, but I miss walking the dogs. I'm in the office most days now so I don't get to see my buddies much. I miss out on all the love. Besides, I think Tim is planning on sitting by the pool tomorrow before you take us sightseeing again. He wants to relax a bit."

Uncle Henry met Mattie's gaze, then faced Lucie. "Sure. If you want. Maybe you can give me some tips."

NO SOONER THAN Lucie closed the bedroom door did Tim point his finger at it. "That woman is not right for him."

Talk about a switch with her being the one talking *him* down. *Heh.* What a trip. One she shouldn't be taking pleasure in, but...oh well.

He paced the small area beside the queen-sized bed before continuing his rant. "And I didn't like the way she deflected the question about where she was from. She made it vague by saying northeast and then changed the subject by saying hello to that Eleanor woman. And she called me *adorable*. Adorable? Really?"

Could he say it any louder? Lucie snapped her fingers. "Tchchch. Pipe down. Henry's right down the hall."

This was starting to not be as fun as she thought. It took so much energy to be the calm, rational one.

Exhausted, she dropped onto the bed and kicked her shoes off. "You might be a wee bit overprotective. She's a nice woman. A little loud and...*bold*, maybe, but she seems crazy about Henry."

Tim stopped pacing, just halted mid-lap, propped his hands on his hips, and speared her with a look. "She's—"

Lucie snapped her hand up and put her finger to her lips. How many times would she have to tell him to be quiet? "Keep it down, fella."

Her cutie-pie detective drew a deep breath through his nose, then exhaled long and slow.

"There you go," she said. "Nice and easy. In and out."

"Right. Sorry. I don't get it though. Totally not his type."

His type. Lucie never bought into people having one. What the heck did that even mean? Just because one person didn't look like the other, didn't mean they weren't compatible. "Maybe that's the point."

When Tim gave her the WTF face, she sighed. "I get you're concerned about your uncle. I love that about you. But he's a grown man. Maybe he's looking for a little...excitement."

"Ha. That's what you're going with?"

"Yes. You said Mattie is the complete opposite of who your aunt was."

"Totally."

"Okay. Think about it, Tim. He's a widower. If he loved your aunt with everything he had, that loss devastated him. His wife would be irreplaceable and being with someone like her would create too many painful memories. Going for someone different might not hurt as much."

Part of this came from experience. Frankie was still very much alive, but he and Tim couldn't be more different. With Tim everything was new, fun, and easy. Other than his fierce protective instincts, there were no similarities. It freed her from making unfair comparisons.

The corner of Tim's mouth lifted into a half-scowl. "I didn't think of it that way."

"You can thank me later."

"I'll do that. But, I'm telling you, my mom will go apeshit. She'll take one look at Mattie and think she's a gold digger."

A familiar tension streamed down Lucie's neck. This was the other thing that made her crazy. All her life, she'd been judged because of her father. As if she was incapable of living a legitimate life. "Well, it's not up to your mom, is it?"

"Try telling her that."

Good point. And Lucie couldn't really fault her for being concerned about her brother's emotional well-being.

"All right, well, let's give this the Joe Rizzo approach."

Tim gawked. "You want me to kill her?"

Hardy-har. "You're charged up right now, so I'll forgive you for that crack. For all his faults, my dad has a way of assessing one's character."

Prison and her father's choice of occupation, something Lucie still hadn't found a way to accept, had blessed him with an uncanny ability to size people up.

Give him two minutes with Mattie and he'd profile her better than any FBI agent. He'd also have the cops on his payroll run a background check. All in a day's work for the man.

"I believe that," Tim said. "When you spend time around the people your dad does, it heightens your senses. I'm a cop. I get that. That's why I don't like her avoiding the details on where she's from. She could be a con-artist jumping from retiree to retiree and cleaning out their back accounts."

"You're really worried about this."

"Hell, yes. I may be paranoid, but I've seen enough situations with seniors getting ripped off that my Spidey-sense is firing."

Worn out from the day, she lifted a hand then let it drop against the bed. "Well, do what my dad does and dig up information on her. Then you'll know."

FOUR

The next morning, Lucie left Tim at Henry's kitchen table with a fresh pot of coffee and his cell phone. No doubt, by the time she returned, he'd have a full work-up on Matilda Mournay.

Outside, she followed Henry to the driveway, lagging behind to enjoy a few seconds of sunshine. He veered around his Lexus to a four-seater golf cart.

"Hop in," he said. "Mattie's place is about half a mile. Sometimes I walk, but I'm tired today. Too much Tiki Night for an old man."

"You're not old."

"For that, I am. Anything more than two drinks and I feel like a bus hit me."

"You had three last night."

"It became a double-decker on that third one."

Lucie laughed. No wonder Tim loved this man.

Henry put the cart in gear and backed out. He cruised along, waving to neighbors out for a late morning stroll or doing yard work.

"Fred," he called to a man loading a paddleboard into

the back of a pickup. "Be careful on that thing. Wear a life vest."

Fred raised a hand in response. Lucie felt a tug of longing for Franklin. Which was saying something, because for years all she wanted was to run from it. Now, as she got older, she appreciated the comfort of knowing everyone on the block. Knowing their eccentricities and habits. Mrs. Delvecchio leaving her garbage cans out long enough that one of the neighbors would bring them in for her. Or the Jamesons flying their W flags on every Cubs' win.

Home.

"Everyone seems so friendly here."

Henry nodded. "For the most part. I'm in a good area. A lot of northerners here, so we all trade stories. Over on the west side are more the local folks. They're snobs. Like they should run the place because they're natives."

That, too, sounded like her hometown, where lifers made sure the new folks understood the parking rules. Meaning, if there was a lawn chair or a garbage can in a spot, the spot was "reserved." In the winter, if you shoveled it, you owned it until the next snowfall. No exceptions.

"I'm assuming Mattie lives on this side?"

"Yes. Right on the border though."

"And where is she from? I don't think she said."

Hey, Tim might have been overreacting, but it couldn't hurt to ask a few questions.

"All over. New Hampshire, Connecticut, Delaware. She migrated down the east coast until she got here."

"Wow. I can't imagine. My parents have lived in the same house for thirty years."

"That was me before I moved here. Forty-five years in my house. I needed a change."

Un-hunh. Just as Lucie expected. "So you moved down here and met Mattie."

"Yep. She's got an adventurous side." He glanced over and smiled. "I'm hoping I can get her to settle down."

"You seem very fond of her."

He hooked a left turn and waved to a couple walking a dog. "Hi, Beth. Ernie. See you at poker night." He came back to Lucie. "After my wife died, part of me went with her. I almost couldn't stand it. Everywhere I looked, something reminded me. And then I met Mattie and—*boom*—I'm like a new man. I have ten years on her, but she doesn't seem to mind. She helped me through the worst of the grief."

"It's wonderful that you found her. Does she have children?"

"No. Never wanted them. She's divorced. Married a Navy man for a few years but couldn't take him being gone so much."

"I've heard it can be difficult."

Henry pulled up to a quaint cottage with an attached garage and a screened lanai jutting out from the back. Yellow and pink flowers bordered the front and a giant potted plant stood near the door, a welcome sign sticking out of the dirt.

Everything about the place felt bright and homey. Well-loved.

"It's pretty," Lucie said.

"My Mattie has great taste."

Of course she did. According to Henry, Mattie might be perfect.

He parked in the driveway and led Lucie up the front path. A loud bark erupted, the deep gravely sound carrying through the door.

Clearly, Aphrodite wasn't the toy poodle Lucie had expected.

"Um, what kind of dog is Aphrodite?"

"Pit bull."

With a name like Aphrodite? All righty then.

"She's okay. Mattie rescued her from the pound. She felt sorry for her. Damned dog is strong as an ox, but once you get to know her she's lovable."

"How is she with strangers?"

"Hit or miss. She's territorial. But she knows me. You'll be fine."

Henry unlocked the door, pushing it open while sliding one knee in to block the dog. More barking, but nothing about it sounded aggressive. It was excited. Once inside with the door shut, Lucie stood in the entryway, allowing Aphrodite, a stunning gray pit bull, to sniff her.

"You can pet her," Henry said. "Good girl, Aphrodite. Stay."

While Aphrodite did her inspection, Lucie took in the living room, a large area with a vaulted ceiling. Breezy black curtains hung on the front windows, blocking any sunshine. If Lucie lived in Florida, she'd have sun streaming in all day.

Still, the room was cozy with two loveseats, a couple upholstered side chairs, and a Persian rug with bursts of red and orange.

After a minute, sensing Aphrodite had settled down, Lucie held the back of her hand out. A few sniffs later—lookie here—the dog gave it a swipe with her tongue. "Yes," Lucie said. "You're a sweet girl. Are you ready for your breakfast?"

The dog's ear flared up. Aphrodite took off running down the hallway, her paws sliding on what looked like

Travertine tile as she made a turn into what may have been the mudroom.

"Now you did it," Henry said. "Cover your ears. She knows that word."

"Breakfast?"

Ah-wooooooo.

Henry angled around Lucie, hustling into the room with Aphrodite. Lucie was fast on his heels, bypassing the kitchen that opened to a small dining area.

In the mudroom, Aphrodite stood next to an elevated double dog bowl, her tail swinging back and forth.

"I'm coming," Henry said. "Relax."

Ah-woooooo. Ah-wooo.

No wonder he'd warned her to cover her ears. As a professional, Lucie should've anticipated something like this. One thing she'd learned the hard way was to never get a dog too hyped up.

"Lucie, while I'm giving her a snack, grab the leash out of the cabinet by the sink. It's in a bowl on the first shelf."

She opened the cabinet to the right of the sink. An envelope—*whoopsie*—and a folded flyer tumbled out of an overstuffed vertical letter organizer on the second shelf. Lucie scooped both items from the granite counter and noted the envelope's smooth linen paper. The ornate lettering on the return address caught her eye. Really, she wasn't snooping.

Not much.

Crawford Academy - Los Angeles, California.

The other was a flyer about the grand opening of a new condo development in Boston.

"Not that one. The other cabinet."

At the sound of Henry's voice, Lucie flinched and quickly finagled the envelope and flyer back into the organizer. "Sorry. They fell out when I opened the cabinet."

"Yeah. No problem. Honest mistake."

It was. But Crawford Academy? In Los Angeles. Why did Mattie have a letter from a school if she had no children. Too bad Lucie hadn't had an extra second to peek inside.

Why would a Florida retiree be interested in Boston? She shook it off. *Bad, Lucie, bad.*

But...Tim. By now, he'd be deep into investigative mode, working his contacts about Mattie Mournay.

Helping the cause. That's all this snooping was. A way to put Tim's mind at ease and save their vacation from further stress.

When she got back to Henry's, she'd do a search on Crawford Academy. Mattie might be an alumna. Heaven knew, Lucie got all sorts of mail from Notre Dame.

Lucie retrieved the leash from the opposite cabinet and handed it to Henry, who waited in the doorway for Aphrodite. "Why don't I wait outside while you two finish up?"

"Sure. We'll be out in two minutes."

Two minutes. More than enough time for a girl to put her thumbs to work on her phone.

"Crawford Academy," Tim said from his spot at Henry's kitchen table.

The low swish of running water through the wall told them Henry was still in the shower washing—as he put it— the dog stink off. In the last twenty-four hours, Henry had showered no less than three times. He was either doing naughty things in there or obsessed over hygiene.

Either way, it gave Lucie time to fill Tim in on her findings.

"That was the name on the envelope. I looked it up. It's a

boarding school in Los Angeles. Three-thousand students at fifty-five thousand per year."

Tim whistled. "Mattie doesn't have any kids. Why is she getting a letter from a boarding school? Did you look inside?"

"Of course not. That's her private business."

Tim rolled his eyes. He knew better. Lucie spent half her life snooping. Her amateur detective antics tended to test the upper limits of his blood pressure.

"Like you've never snooped in private files? What about the whack-job gallery owner?"

Ooh, he just had to go there. A crime had been committed and she'd been implicated. She *had* to snoop. "Totally different, Detective. I was about to become someone's prison bitch. What else was I supposed to do?"

"Prison bitch. Good one."

"And, hello? Your uncle was standing right there. I couldn't rifle through the woman's mail with him hovering."

The lack of response indicated Tim's willingness to concede the point. Lucie waved one hand. "Anyway, Crawford Academy. Could she have gone to school there? Henry said her family moved around a lot."

Tim sat back and crossed his arms across his broad chest. "He never said anything about California."

True. "He said northeast. Shoot."

"According to my search, she's never lived on the west coast. Mostly Connecticut.

Hunh. How the heck was Mattie linked to Crawford Academy? Lucie should've risked it and looked in the envelope. Lost opportunity. For all the stuff she'd pulled in the last year, a little peek hardly ranked in her top ten of illegal offenses. *Next time.* "What else did you find?"

"Nothing. Matilda Mournay is squeaky clean. No arrests, no convictions, not even a speeding ticket."

"Then why are we doing this? Maybe we should stay out of your uncle's business and let him live his life."

"Ha!"

"What?"

"Usually, I'm the one telling you that. I'm seeing it from the other side."

Finally, she wasn't the screwed up one. "It's not fun is it?" Maybe not for him. For her? Loads of fun.

"Hell no."

"If nothing else, you now understand how it feels when a loved-one is involved. It's ten times worse."

Tim sat forward and propped his chin in his hand. Something told Lucie he wasn't about to let Henry's love life go unexplored.

She walked around the table to rest her hand on his shoulder. "Stop worrying. Henry is a big boy. He's in love and we're meddling. It's not fair."

"Can't help it."

"Well, try harder. We're in paradise. Your uncle is happy. Leave it alone and let's have a relaxing visit. Peace, no family drama, and a hot Irish detective. That's all I want."

If nothing else, Tim could be distracted by sex. Lots of it. If it diverted him from interfering in his uncle's life, she'd do it. Happily. Whatever her issues with her family, she never butted into their lives. Her constant attempts to convince Joey that being a bookie wasn't a career only amounted to him being irritated with her. Miss High and Mighty, he'd called her. In the end, it wasn't worth driving a wedge between her and her brother.

People needed to do what they needed to do.

Tim sat up and swiveled sideways, guiding her onto his lap. "You're right. I'm overthinking it."

Ooh, those words must have hurt. She'd refrain from teasing him about it. "Listen, O'Hottie, you promised me time at the pool. Let's move it. I'm ready for a day with zero stress."

"FINALLY."

Lucie tipped her head up, allowing warm sunshine to spill over her cheeks. This was what vacations were meant to be.

Beside her, Tim disrupted her stillness by straightening his beach towel and tucking the corners through the slats, so they wouldn't flap around. He glanced at her, took in the new sapphire two-piece bathing suit Ro talked her into, and waggled his eyebrows. "I like the suit."

The bathing suit, by Ro's standards anyway, was tame and covered most everything, revealing only enough cleavage to make Lucie's petite body look like more than a bag of bones. Thank God for boobs.

Her whale white skin wasn't exactly the thing of sex sirens, but a girl had to start somewhere. By the end of the week? Look out, people. Tan, tan, tan.

Tim straddled his chair and pulled his T-shirt off as he dropped onto it.

My, my, my. Her man's shoulders. Those babies landed somewhere between totally ripped and toned. Lucie caught her breath every time. Every. Time.

She reached into her bag, grabbed SPF fifteen sunscreen, thought about it, and opted for the fifty. This was a job for the big boys. Without it, he'd be redder than his hair in an hour.

"Here you go handsome. I don't want you crispy tonight."

"Thanks."

He started the process of armoring up while peering out at the pool, where patrons circled a swim-up bar.

That was an idea she'd gladly support. "Are you hungry?"

"Yeah. The bar?"

"I'd love it. We'll take a selfie and send it to Ro and Joey."

"It's a plan." He handed her the sunscreen. "Do my back and we'll go."

She squirted a mound of lotion into her hand. *Whoopsie.* She'd protect the entire state with that glob. She swiped a quarter-sized amount onto Tim's back and wiped the rest on her towel. *Blech.*

"Did my uncle tell you he wants us back by two-thirty for sightseeing?"

"He didn't, but that should work. We don't want to be out here too long the first day. Is Mattie coming with us?"

"God, I hope so. I'm insanely curious about that woman."

She finished rubbing in the last of the sunscreen and gave him a light smack. "I know but be careful asking too many questions. Your uncle won't appreciate it. He'll know you're pumping her for information."

Tim sat back, hooked his hands behind his head, and closed his eyes. "I told my mother I'd give her a report. She's driving me crazy with the texts. Insisting on a picture."

Lucie imagined Tim's mother, a woman who opted for nothing shorter than knee-length attire and breezy tops, getting her first look at Mattie's animal print. "Oh, boy."

Tim laughed. "Exactly. She'll freak."

"I'm glad it's your family drama and not mine. I'm enjoying the quiet. I love them, but they're a lot."

"You're telling me?"

She swatted him on the arm without any real force. They both knew this break from the Rizzo crew was much-needed. No sense denying it.

A couple in their late fifties walked past on their way to the pool steps. Tim did his cop thing, watching them as they went, studying their movements.

The couple entered the pool, dodging a group of folks chatting in the shallow end.

Retirement. Lucie would enjoy lazy days of hanging by the pool or beach and visiting with friends. "This place is busy."

Tim nodded. "It's flooded with snowbirds until April. Henry said we'll put our freedom at risk if we save a chair by the pool. If you throw a towel on the chair and don't actually sit, the pool police confiscate your towels."

"No way."

"They had a brawl last month. Fines were handed out, Luce. It was ugly."

"If only those were our problems in Chicago."

"I'd be bored."

As a detective with the Chicago Police Department, Tim saw all kinds of depravity. Some nights he came home laughing, telling her wacky stories too absurd to not be true. Others, as much as he tried to hide his foul mood, she knew whatever had crashed in on him had left its mark. The cases he particularly disliked were crimes against the elderly. Those drove him to madness.

A woman's laughter came from the bar. Time to try it out. Lucie glanced over at Tim. "Let's go to the bar. We'll talk about you retiring and becoming the towel police."

"Amen, babe. Amen."

In the distance, the theme from *The Godfather* sounded from the direction of the parking lot.

Her father was thirteen hundred miles away and reminders of her hometown still chased her. "It never ends," she said.

"Hey! Knock it off," came a woman's shout from the same general direction.

Was that? Half-paralyzed, Lucie held Tim's gaze.

Couldn't be.

"Relax," Tim said. "Uncle Henry sends me pictures of tricked out golf carts. It's a thing down here. Some have custom horns. A friend of his paid thirty thousand a few months back."

Thirty thousand dollars. On a golf cart.

"Woohoo!" the woman's voice sounded again, this time closer and...Oh. My. *God.*

That voice. Still paralyzed, Lucie couldn't move. She simply sat, gaze pinned to Tim's face as he looked beyond her, and his amused smile slowly disintegrated. And then, there it was.

The horror.

Locked jaw, hard eyes, stiff posture.

"Woohoo! We're here!"

Lucie shook her head hard enough to dislodge something. That's what she needed. The part of her brain that registered current action to fall out of her head.

"Tim, tell me I've gone insane and that the voice I just heard is in my head. It's not real." She waggled a hand. "I'm hallucinating it's Roseanne, who should, at this very moment, be manning the phones at our office."

"Woohoo!"

Dammit, if she never heard a woohoo again she'd die happy.

Refusing to look, she focused on Tim. "You're not answering."

What the hell was wrong with him? Probably the same thing wrong with her. The two of them stunned stupid.

"Luce! O'Brien! What kind of greeting is that?"

Oh no. *That* voice was definitely not her imagination. That one had tormented her since the day she popped out of her mother.

"Shut it, Joey. We just got here and already you're starting."

Every head in the pool turned and if Lucie needed further confirmation, a few male jaws dropped. *Boom.* Just hung open.

"How bad is it?" Lucie asked. "I'm terrified to look."

Tim puffed out his cheeks and exhaled long and slow.

That bad.

Courage summoned, Lucie swung around. Roseanne strutted toward her wearing a red bikini top straining to keep her 36Ds from battling their way free. She'd tied a black sarong around her waist, but what was the point? It revealed enough leg to almost be obscene. Behind Ro, Joey trudged along, flipping off the ogling men in the pool.

Lucie faced Tim. "It's really not a nightmare, is it? This is happening."

"It is," Tim said. "And Luce?"

"What?"

"It just got worse."

Was that even possible at this point? She closed her eyes, readied herself for whatever it was. "Tell me."

"Your dad just walked in."

FIVE

"**S**urprise!" Ro said, excitement bringing her voice a full octave higher.

Shock—and maybe a touch of outrage because, holy hell, her family had just hijacked her vacation—held Lucie captive on her lounger.

On the other side of Tim, Joey tossed a couple beach towels on the empty chair meant for Uncle Henry. Hands on hips, Joey perused the pool. The swim-up bar, the cascading waterfall in the corner, the hot tub.

"Ooh, hot tub. My back is killing me. I'm going in."

"Go right ahead," Tim said. "Make yourself at home."

Never one to let sarcasm slip by, Joey nodded. "Gee, thanks, O'Brien. I will."

Joey yanked off his pristine white T-shirt that Mom had probably ironed for him, sort of folded it, and dropped it on the edge of the chair.

"Baby girl," Dad hollered from two feet away, "we made it."

Beside him, Mom waved furiously. "Hi, Lucie. Hi, Tim. We wanted to surprise you. Are you? Gosh, this is fun."

Oh, they were. Tim's flaming red ears indicated he might be something else also.

"Fun," he muttered.

Lucie had suffered through nightmare Rizzo situations before. Dad's arrest and trial. Visiting him in prison. Finding out her saint of a mother had an affair with the town butcher. All of it cemented in her mind, serving as a reminder that life as a mob boss's daughter might be easier from thousands of miles away. At least until they all showed up.

Unbelievable. And who the hell was manning the office? Ready to spew, Lucie looked up at Ro, who'd just whipped off her sarong and flashed a whole lot of skin. Talk about a Brazilian Wax. Holy moly.

Even with the three pounds she'd just lost, the remaining ten she'd gained had strategically landed on her butt. The one barely hidden under her so-called bathing suit masquerading as a few swatches of material.

To say that sucker left little to the imagination wouldn't be an understatement. It would be a straight-up travesty. Considering the average age in that pool, someone better bust out the CPR kit. God only knew the last time this much skin had been on display in Paradise City.

Finally, Lucie's outrage bubbled, shooting her from her spot. She hopped up, about to rip into her BFF, but the look on Ro's face, the delight and...hope, knocked the roiling tip of Lucie's anger off.

Shoot. They'd totally intruded, and she was having trouble being mad? Really?

Ro hugged her. "Please don't be mad. We wanted all of us to take a trip together."

Dammit.

Lucie lifted her arms, wrapped them around Ro and

gave her a squeeze. Seven months ago, she'd have felt bone. Now, after regular meals at Mom and Dad's—and Joey "liking a little meat on her"—her BFF had filled out. A topic never far from any of their minds, since Ro couldn't stop blaming Mom for her lot in life. Over the months, it turned into a game: Ro complaining about the weight, but not really working all that hard to get rid of it.

Family. Go figure.

"Cannonball!"

Joey's voice. Oh no. A loud splash and a bunch of yelling started, and Lucie swung back.

"Yeah," Tim said. "He just did that into the hot tub. He's lucky he didn't break his foot."

Total nightmare.

Ro flapped her arms, sending her boobs bouncing. "Joey! You're *such* an animal."

"I don't know where he learned to behave this way," Mom said.

"Good one," Dad hollered.

Of course. Lucie gritted her teeth. "Mystery solved."

Mom made a humming noise. She'd taken up meditation lately—a last ditch effort to not murder someone—and the former came with her new Zen attitude. She breathed deep and faced Dad. "Joe, you really shouldn't encourage him. This isn't Franklin. It's peaceful here."

"*Was* peaceful," Tim added.

Now that the initial trauma had worn off, they'd get down to it, because half of Lucie's staff was in Florida.

She held up two hands. "I don't want to be the wet blanket in all this, but, hey, you know me, I have to ask. Who's manning Coco Barknell?"

Ro moved to the empty lounger and started spreading one of the towels across it. "Mrs. R, you sit, we'll find more chairs. And, Luce, we have it all worked out. We hired a temp for the phones and gave the part-timers extra hours. Honestly, it's a slow weekend for dog walking, so it all worked out. Joey and I fly home Monday morning."

"Lucie," Mom said. "Please. We wanted to surprise you. When's the last time we all had a vacation together?"

Years. That's how long. Before her father wound up doing a two-year stint for tax evasion.

Looking at her mother's heart-shaped face and hazel eyes that sometimes, like now, appeared green, Lucie caved. What else could she do? Throwing a tantrum would ruin the day completely. How was it that her family barged in on her time with Tim and *she* wound up feeling bad?

She turned, giving her back to her family and Ro, and faced Tim, on his feet behind her. One thing about her man, he always stood to greet people. A good man. That was Tim.

Manners aside, the tightness behind his half-smile gave him away. Bless him for trying, but make no mistake, Tim was not happy.

He leaned in and kissed the top of her head. "All good." He faced her dad. "Joe, have you guys eaten? My uncle says the food from the bar is decent. How about we grab a table?"

No nasty looks. No pouting. No cold shoulder. Oh, this man. She'd be crazy not to marry him. She poked him square in the chest. "You're a rockstar."

To that, he leaned in again, got right up to her ear. "Believe me, you'll make it up to me."

The threat fell flat, as it always did, because she usually enjoyed making it up to him more than he did. *Go, Lucie.*

While Tim and Dad left to commandeer a table, Lucie faced Ro and Mom. "I'll say this, you all know how to make an entrance."

Mom made a huffing noise. "Wait'll you see the golf cart. It's almost embarrassing."

Ro snorted. "Stop. You know you laughed when you saw it."

"You were *The Godfather* theme, weren't you?"

Ro paddled her hands. "Yes! So fun. Come on, I'll show you." She scooped up her sarong again and hooked it around her waist. Thank goodness, because the men in the pool could now go back to their conversation and Joey wouldn't have to threaten anyone.

"I'm hungry," Mom said. "Meet me at the table. I'm ordering a pitcher of rum punch. And I'm not sharing."

As they walked, Lucie grabbed hold of Ro's elbow and pinched. Not hard, but enough for her BFF to know she had an issue with their little surprise.

"Ouch," Ro said, her voice completely level and lacking any heat.

"Please. That didn't hurt."

"I figured I should at least make an effort."

Lucie couldn't help it. She laughed. "I should throttle you. I finally get a vacation with Tim and you crash. What the hell is wrong with you?"

"Well, in my own defense, I tried to talk them out of it. Joey, of all people, thought of it. Blurted it out over dinner last week. I tried, Luce, I really did, but you know your family. They're tough."

"Ya think?"

"Besides, you should be thanking me."

She couldn't wait to hear this one.

"At first, they were going to follow you to the Keys. Then I suggested maybe your mom and dad stay here for the week. Check the place out as a retirement option. This could have been *so* much worse. Think about it, Luce. You,

Tim, and all of us on your romantic Keys vacation. Mmm, mmm, *mmm*. That would have been something."

Horror washed over Lucie. They'd definitely dodged a bullet. "Thank you. I think."

"You're welcome."

At the exit, an older man with a cane came through the gate and, apparently mesmerized by Ro's hard-to-contain boobs, halted. His lips parted slightly. If he started drooling, Lucie would lose it. Absolutely meltdown.

"Old man," Ro said. "Quit staring at my titties. If you were younger, I'd slap you."

Lordy!

"They're so pretty," the man said.

Ro shooed the man away. "You know it. Now move along. Show is over. And when I come back, don't let my boyfriend catch you staring. He's an animal. No controlling him."

"Okay. My wife will be here by then anyway."

"Excellent," Ro waved Lucie to follow her to the parking lot. "It's a shame men don't grow out of being pigs."

"He's a hundred and ten. He probably hasn't seen this kind of action in forty years."

Ro looked over at her, a huge smile in place. "I do love you, Luce." She gestured to a row of parked carts. "We're over here. I found this little number online. Did you know they have a rental service down here? I could totally see Joey and your dad owning something like that."

"Except the first complaint would wind up with them all rolling on the ground throwing punches."

Ro tilted her head one way, then the other. "Something to consider for sure. But Joey is getting better. Your dad? Who knows? Never mind that, close your eyes."

Oh, now she was pushing the boundaries of friendship. "I'm not in the mood for games, Ro."

"*Ssshhh.* Close them."

Lucie snapped her eyes closed. Some battles weren't worth fighting. Ro held her arm, guiding her a few steps before positioning her. A little to the right, a bit to the left.

"Any time now, Ro."

"Watch your step. Okay. Open 'em."

Lucie did as she was told and laid eyes on a shiny black Escalade. Well, the golf cart version of it, complete with replica Cadillac headlights and the logo on the front grill. Chrome rims gleamed bright enough to light Chicago during a blackout.

God, that thing. So gaudy.

Lucie burst out laughing. Only her family.

Ro did a fast clap and squealed. "I know. It looks just like mine. And the horn is programable. I thought Papa Joe might not like *The Godfather*, but I went for it."

"And?"

"He laughed."

"Of course he did. He loves you."

Lord knew Ro got away with just about anything with Dad. The two of them shared a twisted logic on all things ranging from politics to meatballs.

Ro stepped forward and draped herself across the front of the cart. "Later, you gotta take a picture of all of us in this thing. I wish I could have this in Chicago. Picture me driving to the office in this baby? Ha!"

That would be a sight. It ranked right up there with Joey riding one of the scooters Lucie purchased to get around the city faster. The minute the mob guys down at Petey's saw it, they all took turns riding. The golf cart might put them over the edge.

Ro straightened up and gave it a light pat. "Anyhoo, how's the trip going so far?"

Lucie hooked her arm through Ro's. "Before you all crashed it? It's been great. It makes me realize how hard we've been working this past year. Ro, we have to force each other to take vacations. The minute I stepped out of the airport and felt warm air, my stress level dropped."

"You needed it, Luce. And what about Tim? How's his uncle?"

"Such a nice man. I swear, Tim's family is disgustingly normal."

Ro curled her lip. "What fun is that?"

"There *is* a bit of a shake-up with Uncle Henry's girlfriend."

"That devil has a squeeze?"

"She's taking the straight-laced Uncle Henry to the dark side. It's kinda refreshing." Lucie held both hands over her head. "Big hair, big boobs, tight clothes."

"Oh, my God. She's me."

Lucie bumped Ro as they strolled. "That's what I said. You in twenty-five years, anyway. She seems like a nice lady. Maybe a bit of an attention seeker is all. Tim's freaking out. His mother wants an update on Mattie and he's ignoring her. I guess Henry's late wife was basically a nun. Poor Tim doesn't know what to do."

"It's none of her business."

"I told him that. He still spent the morning running a background check on Mattie."

The drama queen threw her head back and gasped. "People! I swear I can't stand it. I'm going to live on an island by myself."

Good luck with that. A week without designer shoes and Ro would shrivel up and die. "In Tim's defense, there's something off about her. She's too squeaky clean. Not even a parking ticket."

"Well, not everyone grew up like us, Luce. Law abiding citizens do exist."

Ro's family didn't have a criminal history, but they weren't adverse to buying items that, as they say in Franklin, fell off a truck. Meaning, they were hotter than August in Arizona.

Ro's working theory was she got a good deal. Like going to the outlet mall.

Up ahead, a couple exited the pool, arguing over someone being rude. Had to be Joey. Had to be.

Lucie offered a smile as the couple moved past then focused back on her own conversation with Ro. "This morning I helped Henry walk Mattie's dog. While there I saw an envelope from a boarding school in California."

"So?"

"*So*, Henry told us she doesn't have any kids."

"Maybe it was a solicitation. You know spam snail mail."

"That she kept in her kitchen cabinet? She would have thrown it out if it was junk."

Ro shrugged. "It could be a friend's kid. Maybe they're pen pals."

Now she was reaching. "Pen pals? Why waste a stamp? Send an email. It's faster."

They entered the pool area and Lucie pointed to the bar. "They're over here."

Ro nodded. "What's Tim's plan?"

"I don't think he has one. He'll need to come up with something, though, because his mom isn't giving up. Even if he ignores her while we're here, he's toast—burnt toast— when he gets home. She'll be all over him."

Still arm in arm, they strolled along the side, passing small groups of folks milling in the water, chatting with friends. A woman's laughter, then a splash drew Lucie's eye to a man who'd just ambushed the laughing woman with a kiss.

Twenty years from now Lucie wanted that. Clear blue skies, warm sunshine, and Tim. *Goals, Luce. Goals.*

"All right," Ro said. "Let's think about this. She has no criminal history, but that doesn't mean anything. Maybe she just hasn't gotten caught."

"At what?"

"Whatever her scam is."

How the heck did they go from no criminal history to Mattie being a scammer? Ro's mind. Scary place. "Who said she has one?"

Ro gave her a massive eye roll. "Is Henry rich? Maybe she's one of those con-women who prey on widowed men. The old Sweetheart Scam." Ro pulled her arm free from Lucie's and made a fishing motion. "She lures him in and then—*bam*—bleeds him dry. We really should look into this."

Now her, too? "No. It's Henry's life. He's happy. I shouldn't have said anything."

"Look, O'Hottie has good instincts. If he's suspicious, there might be something to it." Ro waved a hand. "Introduce me to this woman. I'll figure it out."

"Roseanne!"

Joey. He must have given up on the hot tub and opted for the pool.

Ro propped her hands on her hips and whipped around. "Stop that screaming."

Oh, boy. Lucie kept her gaze on Tim, sitting at a table for six not ten feet in front of them and chatting it up with Dad, whose hands flew as he spoke.

"Order me food," Joey hollered.

Ro gave him a thumbs up. "He's a Neanderthal, but I love him."

"Baby girl," Dad said, "I'm having grouper. And it's fried. Your mother is upset."

"She'll forgive you. Might as well enjoy your vacation, Dad."

Tim waved Lucie to the vacant chair beside him. "Luce, your dad and I were just discussing the merits of castration. He's in favor."

I don't even want to know.

"Excellent," she said. "What did you order for lunch?"

"Nothing yet." He grinned. "I waited for you."

Mom made her way back to the table, a pitcher of a colorful beverage in hand. The rum punch, no doubt. Mom was going all in.

"Roseanne, I ordered Joey chicken wings. It comes with fries."

Mom. Always taking care of her baby boy.

"Perfect," Ro said. "He'll love it. I'm not eating."

Sure she wasn't.

"Here we go," Mom, Dad, and Tim all said.

Ro's hunger strikes often lasted long enough for Mom to slice a pound cake.

Lucie perused the menu sitting in the middle of the table. "You can split a chicken wrap with me. We'll skip the cheese."

"Ooh. That sounds good," Ro said.

Tim laughed. At least he found the humor in having his vacation crashed.

"O'Hottie," Ro said, "when do we get to meet your uncle and this scammer he's dating?"

SIX

"What scammer?" Mom wanted to know.

Lucie scrunched her nose and looked over at Tim, who gave her the hard, steady look of a man who'd need good, hot sex before forgiving her.

It wouldn't be a hardship.

"You gotta be kidding me," he said.

Lucie smacked the menu on the table. "Hey, I'm sorry. She's my best friend. And I didn't call Mattie a scammer. That was Ro."

"Blah, blah." Ro waved a hand, her French manicure glowing in the sunlight. "Scammer or not, when do we meet her?"

Tim shrugged. "Guessing soon since we're all probably having dinner together."

Dinner. Oh no. Uncle Henry wanted to take them sight-seeing and then to his favorite restaurant. Now they'd have four extra people and who knew if Uncle Henry would appreciate the, um...quirks...of Lucie's family.

"It better be someplace good," Dad said. "I don't eat in crummy restaurants."

"Speaking of Uncle Henry." Tim pointed over Lucie's shoulder.

She angled back to see Henry striding toward them. Even in the midday heat, his long navy shorts and crisp white button-down appeared freshly pressed. Unrumpled, as usual.

"Hello," he said, reaching the table with a bright smile that showed off his tan. "You made friends already?"

Ha. Friends.

"Uncle Henry," Tim said, "this is Joe and Theresa Rizzo. Lucie's parents. And the maniac on the end is Roseanne, Lucie's closest friend. She dates Lucie's brother, Joey." Tim jerked his thumb. "He's in the pool."

Henry's eyebrows hitched.

Tim gave him a sarcastic smile. "And, no, we didn't know they were coming."

"Huh." Henry's green eyes sparkled. "Isn't that nice?"

Hellos and handshakes were exchanged, and Lucie pointed to the empty chair beside her. "Sit, Henry. We're ordering lunch."

"I can't. Mattie just called. Her car broke down forty minutes from here and she needs a ride. I'm on my way to get her, but Aphrodite needs to be fed and walked again in an hour."

"We'll do it," Tim said a little too fast.

Henry's head snapped to him. "I hate to ask."

"You didn't. I offered. Happy to help."

Now, he was laying it on thick. Tim was a good man, an exceptional one really, but this had nothing to do with his character. Walking Mattie's dog meant access to her home.

And if Lucie knew her inquisitive detective boyfriend, he might be snooping while they were inside.

STILL IN HER white swimsuit cover-up and smelling like coconuts, Lucie led Tim through Mattie's front door. Aphrodite leaped up, throwing herself against Lucie and knocking her back a full step. Seeing the dog's launch angle, Tim slid behind Lucie and kept her from going over.

"Off." Lucie put a little alpha, I'm-in-charge in the command, but the dog leaped again. "Why does that always work for Joey and not me?"

"Uh, maybe because he's more than a foot taller and weighs at least two-twenty?"

Once Lucie was steady, Tim stepped around her, body blocking the dog and claiming the space enough that Aphrodite took the hint and sat. Territorial or not, the dog knew Tim had just elected himself pack leader.

Showoff.

Lucie grunted. "I'll feed her."

Aphrodite trotted alongside her as Lucie entered the mudroom. After yesterday's frenzy, she made sure not to mention the B word. Particularly since this was lunch.

"While I feed her, grab the leash out of the cabinet near the sink. The one on the left."

"Is that where you found the envelope?"

An iron fist gripped Lucie's stomach. She'd known all along Tim wanted to snoop. Knowing it and hearing it were two different things.

"Come on. Really? This is your uncle's girlfriend. He loves her. You can't rifle through the woman's stuff."

"Sure I can. It's not like I'm going to steal it. And, when you let someone into your house, you gotta know it's a risk."

Oh, please. *Nice try, detective.* "I didn't snoop the first time I was in your house."

Tim eyed her.

"Well, not totally."

"Exactly. Now where's the envelope?"

Her man obviously wasn't going to give up on this. Rather than have him look through every cabinet and really violate the woman's privacy, she pointed. "The one on the right. Middle shelf. I don't agree with this, Tim."

"Noted." He opened the first cabinet, grabbed the leash and tossed it to her. "Walk the dog while I do my thing."

He slid on a pair of plastic gloves he'd swiped from the bartender at the pool and opened the cabinet. A second later, he'd snatched up the stack of envelopes and flipped through them. Unbelievable.

"The fact that you're wearing gloves is a good indicator you shouldn't be doing this."

"You gonna tell?"

She just might. "*Whatever.* Aphrodite and I will be gone about twenty minutes. If you get caught, you're on your own."

"Once again, noted."

Aphrodite appeared in the mudroom doorway, spotted the leash, and pounced.

"Down." Lucie held her hand out just as the dog landed at her feet, swatting at her toes in some sort of excited dance. "Silly, girl."

She clipped the leash on and led Aphrodite out the front door, leaving Tim to his nefarious activities.

Without question, he'd lost his mind. In the past, she may have been a wee bit obsessed with what Tim called her screwball investigations—dogjackings, restaurant fires, art fraud—but those were isolated incidents where she'd been accused of wrongdoing. Lucie had needed to prove her innocence. And she'd done it.

This? This was nuts and completely unmotivated.

Aphrodite stopped in front of the neighbor's house. "I don't know, Aphrodite. Something about your mom is off, but I don't like invading her privacy."

The dog squirted on the tree, then peered up at Lucie, obviously hoping for recognition. Lucie gave her a vigorous rub behind the ears and added a nuzzle. "Good girl. You're so smart." This earned Lucie a lick or five. Apparently, Aphrodite had accepted her. She moved in for another nuzzle with a kicker of baby talk. "So sweet, you are. Yes, you are."

Ready to continue on, Aphrodite moved toward the next tree. Whoever leash trained this girl did a decent job. Not even a hint of pulling. Made walks so much more pleasant.

The hum of a car engine lifted Lucie's gaze to a black SUV cruising down the block. She recognized the front end as a Lincoln. One of the guys at Petey's had the same model.

Two men sat in the front seat. Were they staring at her? Did the driver just slow down? She'd already been dogjacked—several times—and was in no mood for that. She could also be paranoid. After the ninja bitches had been snatched, she tended to take the security of her clients to another level. One that rivaled Secret Service protection.

"And me without my pepper spray."

She gripped the leash and Aphrodite's ears went straight back.

That fast, Lucie's energy shot right through the leash and put her on edge. Dog trainers worldwide would be horrified. She exhaled, rolled her shoulders and loosened her grip.

No tension, no tension, no tension.

"We're fine, girlfriend. Keep moving."

Lucie made eye contact with the man in the passenger seat. Dark slicked back hair, mid-thirties. Paranoid or not, at least she had a description. Something told her these guys were up to no good. Being a mob princess, she recognized suspicious behavior.

The SUV passed, and Lucie glanced over her shoulder. Brake lights.

"Oh no."

Aphrodite's head whipped around. Damned energy. *Breathe, breathe, breathe.*

The passenger door flew open and the dark-haired guy jumped out. Tall and broad-shouldered, he ran straight at her. Again? Seriously? Did she have a neon "dogjack me" sign over her head?

Well, this guy could screw off. Pepper spray or not, she would *not* let him take this dog. No way.

Run.

Lucie dropped the leash and burst into a sprint. "Run, Aphrodite!"

With the man's longer legs, he'd catch Lucie in a heartbeat, but Aphrodite had a chance. A rock solid one. "Run, girl. Go!"

Aphrodite shot off, her powerful legs creating enough distance that the man would never catch her. "Good girl."

Lucie pumped her legs, pushing hard, but...*ach*. A giant hand landed on her shoulder, pulling her back.

"No! Help! Help! Aaaaahhhhh!"

The piercing scream did nothing, zippo, for her. Jeez, who was this guy?

Panic exploded, sending a blood rush that blurred Lucie's vision. She broke free, started running, her feet slamming the pavement hard enough to jar her back. At least until two long arms locked around her from behind and lifted her off her feet.

No, no, no.

Arms trapped, she kicked downward, managing to connect with the guy's shin.

"Ow. Dammit," he said. "Quit that and you won't get hurt."

Sure. Right. As if she'd believe that.

"Help! Someone! Please! Tim!"

Seriously? What kind of neighborhood watch did these people have when a girl could get snatched right off the street.

Not happening.

Every self-defense tip she'd heard streamed through her mind. No second location. That was the biggie. If this guy got her into the car and took her somewhere, she'd most likely die.

And Joe Rizzo's kid wasn't going out that way. Not on vacation.

She kicked again. "Oh, someone's getting hurt. But it won't be me."

"Ow."

Kick, kick, kick. Damned flip-flops didn't make for a great weapon, but she'd keep at it until her toes broke.

Then she started screaming again, employing that high-pitched wail from childhood she'd use on Joey when he tormented her.

That thing could summon wolves.

The man dragged her toward the car and she kicked again. And again. Mattie's neighbor, a beefy older guy in a T-shirt and shorts, opened his front door. Finally.

She should be dead by now.

Her relief came in a hard burst, but she kicked again.

Just to show this joker who was in charge. Even if she was two feet off the ground.

"Hey!" The neighbor bolted from his small porch. "Let her go. I just called 911."

Cops. Excellent.

Suddenly, more people filed from their homes. One guy carried a baseball bat. It reminded Lucie of the ones Joey and Dad kept in their trunks.

"Lucie!"

Tim's voice. Oh, thank God. The guy held on, dragging her toward the SUV, so she kicked again.

"Ow! Stop that."

"Whatever, dude. You're going down."

More shouts came from people suddenly filling the street and...wait. What was that? Music.

O Sole Mio.

"We're coming, Luce!"

Oh. My. God.

Lucie wrenched her head around, peering down the block. Three houses away the Escalade golf cart carrying Ro, Dad, and Joey closed in.

Fast.

From behind the wheel, Ro hit the horn again, unfurling another chorus of *O Sole Mio*. She'd already changed the damned horn since the pool.

"Baby girl," Dad shouted.

With the golf cart still in motion, Joey hopped off, his big body moving easily into a run toward her.

"Now you're screwed," Lucie said. "That's my brother. He's a maniac."

"Get your hands off my sister!"

Joey drew closer, looming large. Who knew, with his size, he could move that fast?

The guy tossed her. Just hurled her in Joey's path. She crumpled to the ground, her knees taking the brunt of the sidewalk. *Ach.* That hurt. They'd be a mess now. On vacation. When she'd planned on wearing shorts and dresses.

Dirty. Bastard.

But Joey. Yikes. Roaring straight at her too fast to avoid a collision.

"Whoa." She rolled sideways, clearing the way before he leaped over her. "Jerk," she yelled at the SUV guy.

Ooh, she hoped she bruised him for a month.

The passenger door of the SUV flew open and he hopped in. He looked back at her and pointed. "Tell your mother Paul knows where she is."

My mother? What did she have to do with anything?"

Lord, if this was another Butcher Bob deal, Lucie would lose any sanity she had left. Her not-so-saintly mother could be forgiven for one transgression. Two was pushing it.

Then they were gone, roaring down the street. Tim, coming from that direction, ran straight at it, but the driver sped up.

Lucie scrambled to her feet. "Tim! No! Out of the—"

The vehicle whipped to the left, swerving into the wrong lane, barely missing him. Tim reached for the handle, but slipped and stumbled, giving the driver a second to hit the gas.

Joey rattled off some numbers and letters, then repeated it as he typed something into his phone. "Got it."

License plate. Please, let it be.

Ro zoomed up, hitting the brake on the golf cart so hard Dad flew forward in his seat, coming halfway out before grabbing the roof rail to stop his momentum.

"Whoa," Dad said. "Are you nuts or what?"

Joey flapped his arms. "Roseanne! You nearly killed him."

"Well," she said, "I was *trying* to save your sister. Besides there should be seat belts in these damned things."

Tim ran to Lucie, throwing his arms around her, squeezing tight. "Luce, I'm sorry. I didn't hear you. I'm so sorry."

She let out a hard breath. "I'm okay," she said.

He rested his chin on top of her head then kissed the spot. "What happened?"

"I don't know. They just drove up and I thought they were trying to steal Aphrodite."

Tim scanned the area. "Where is she? Did they get her?"

"No. I sent her running off."

"On it," the neighbor said. "We'll put the word out. The community patrol will pick her up." He turned and threw his arms wide. "Everyone fan out. Find that dog!"

The residents retreated. Some on foot, a few in carts, others in cars in search of Aphrodite.

Lucie backed away from Tim, but needing his solid presence, stayed hooked under his arm. She faced her family. "Where's Mom?"

"Still at the pool," Joey said. "She's reading. We figured we'd drive over and give you a lift back. Who the hell was that guy?"

"I have no idea. He said to tell Mom that Paul knows where she is."

Joey turned to Dad. "Paul? Who's that?"

"I don't know. But we're gonna find out right now." Dad whipped out his phone, held it a full arm's length away. "Jesus Christmas, I forgot my glasses." He handed it to Joey. "Call her."

Shaking his head, Joey tapped the screen and held the phone in front of him. Two rings in, Mom picked up the call.

"What is it?" she asked, by way of greeting.

"It's me. Joey."

As if the woman who called her only son "my sweet boy"—gag—wouldn't know his voice?

"Joseph, why are you calling on your father's phone? What happened now?"

Poor Mom. When it came to Dad, there was always something.

"Forget that. Do you know someone named Paul?"

"Paul? Well, there's the one who owns the deli on Franklin Avenue. The Patrones. Nicest people in the world. They always give me free pickles."

Probably because of Dad's reputation. Let's keep the mob boss happy by giving his wife free food.

In the distance, a siren sounded. Had to be the cops the neighbor had called. "Uh," Lucie said, "I'm guessing it's not the Patrones."

"What is she talking about? You know, all I wanted was a few days of peace."

"Hey! It's not my fault."

"Boo-hoo," Joey said. "Someone just tried to snatch her."

Three seconds of silence ensued while Mom processed what Joey said. Any second now she'd fly into her motherly concern and pepper her with questions. Might as well head that off.

"I'm fine. But the guy said to tell my mother Paul knows where she is."

"I have no idea what that means." Mom gasped. "What if it's mistaken identity? I see that all the time on the crime shows. Next thing you know, someone is dead. D-E-A-D."

Lucie rolled her eyes at Tim, but he was too busy staring at the phone, thinking face firmly in place.

Please. He couldn't be buying into this.

"She might not be far off," he said.

Lucie grunted, only to have him hold out a hand. "You were walking in the neighborhood. Maybe they thought you were someone else."

"I don't like it," Dad said. "This Mattie. It was her dog. Does she have a daughter?"

Mattie as the target? The thought might put an already suspicious red-haired detective over the edge.

Lucie patted air. Time to quiet the crazies. "Hold on there, Dad. Let's not make assumptions. We don't need conspiracy theories. Besides, Mattie doesn't have kids."

Ro clucked her tongue. "She could be lying."

And another one. So much for calming the crazies.

A patrol car with lights and sirens at full blast screeched around the corner. Took them long enough. If they'd relied on Paradise City's finest, she'd be a corpse by now.

"Okay," Tim said. "Everyone stay quiet. Let me do the talking. Please."

Ha. Good luck there. He'd been to this rodeo before. He knew the havoc this crew could create.

The cruiser came to a stop and a middle-aged cop slid out. Before he got too close, Tim raised a hand. "I'm Tim O'Brien. Chicago PD. I'm down here visiting my uncle. I don't have my creds on me. We were at the pool."

The cop eyed them, stealing a glance at everyone's hands. *No weapons here, officer.*

"We got a call about a possible abduction?"

Tim waved Lucie over. "Yeah. My girlfriend. This is Lucie Riz—"

"Hi." Lucie cut him off before he could say her last

name. Who knew if folks down here were aware of her Dad's reputation. This was already a visit to Looneyville without throwing that into the mix.

"Ma'am," the cop said, "are you hurt?"

"No. He grabbed me while I was walking the dog. He ran off when he drew a crowd."

"Did you get a look at him?"

"I did."

She offered a brief description plus the license plate number Joey had memorized and found herself the recipient of a slew of questions regarding her assailant's speech patterns, possible tattoos, or identifiable marks. Satisfied he'd ascertained what he could, the cop stepped away to put out a BOLO while the five of them waited on the sidewalk. After finishing his radio call, he pulled Lucie to the side under the watchful eye of her crew.

"BOLO is out. Do you have any idea why you were targeted?"

Lucie forced herself to stand still. To not rock back on her heels and keep her body language neutral. "None. We're here on vacation."

"Un-hunh. Whose dog were you walking?"

The way he asked, that little inflection in his voice sparked something deep in Lucie's gut. As Joe Rizzo's kid, she'd learned to recognize skepticism in cops.

"You think I'm making this *up*? There were no less than twenty people who saw it. Ask any one of them."

"Didn't say that."

Great. Sure. Right. Whatever. Lucie pointed to Mattie's house. "Mattie Mournay. She lives in that house. She's a friend of Tim's uncle and needed help walking her dog, Aphrodite."

"Baby girl," Dad called, "you need me?"

Oh, right. With his temper and mistrust of cops, no telling what might happen. Dad liked to tell people he hated law enforcement, but he had plenty of them on his payroll. And he seemed to like Tim well enough.

Which was good considering Lucie might be popping out baby O'Brien's.

Oy. Vey.

She held up a hand. "I'm good, Dad. Thanks."

"All right," the cop said. "We'll look into this. With the plate, we should find him quick. Stay close to your phone. We might have more questions."

"Of course. I'm not going anywhere, and I certainly have nothing to hide."

That I know of.

It took ninety minutes to corral Aphrodite and return her home, where she was now tucked into her bed sleeping off her jaunt. After showering, Lucie and Tim sat at Uncle Henry's table sipping lemonade. Well, Tim was alternating between that and a water bottle. Her man wasn't a big fan of lemonade unless it was laced with vodka, which he might need at the moment.

He drummed his thumb against the table. "You know what I'm thinking, right?"

With him, it could be any number of things, but she had a pretty good idea. "The boarding school?"

"You look young. You're tiny and he saw you from the back. Maybe he thought you were a teenager."

As much as Lucie hated it, on her best day, after consuming a large meal, she might hit a hundred and ten pounds. If she was bloated.

From behind, she'd easily be mistaken as younger. Particularly with her hair in a ponytail. Tim's theory wasn't far off.

"It does seem an odd coincidence someone sees me with

Mattie's dog and references my mother. Still, we can't accuse her of anything. I've spent my life being judged unfairly and it's no fun."

"For God's sakes, Luce, I'm not gonna waterboard her."

From outside, the slam of a car door sounded.

Henry.

A sick feeling overtook her. How would they even explain this? Peering down the hall to the front door, she let out a long breathy sigh. "Sounds like he's here."

"Yeah. Won't this be fun?"

It wasn't every day a man got to question his beloved uncle regarding his girlfriend's possibly shady life.

"Just go easy on him. It'll be a shock to him, too."

"I know."

They rose and headed for the living room, reaching it just as the door opened and Henry strode through.

With Mattie.

Oh, come on!

Mattie's presence tripped everything up.

So, Mattie, are you lying about your lack of children? So, Mattie, why are you getting letters from a private school in California? So, Mattie, who's Paul and why is he after you?

"Crap," Tim muttered a wee bit too loud.

Quicker on her feet than even she'd anticipated, Lucie forced a bright smile. "Hello, you two."

Ugh. The greeting packed way too much high-pitched sweetness. Uncle Henry stared at her like she might be stoned.

Maybe she needed to tone that down.

"Helloooo," Mattie said, clearly missing tension tight enough to strangle an elephant. "We just stopped at the house and my baby is sleeping soundly. Thank you for wearing her out. She loves her walks."

She did a whole lot more than walk.

When Lucie failed to respond, Tim's elbow connected with hers, shooting her out of her mind travel. "Uh, right, sure. No problem. She's a sweet girl. I, um, brought Tim with me."

As segues went, it wasn't great, but heck, it had been a long couple hours. It would have to do. All eyes shifted to Tim. His sunburned skin deepened to a shade darker and a sheen of sweat peppered his forehead. Holy cow, Lucie had never seen him sweat like that under pressure.

Uncle Henry rolled his bottom lip out as he studied his nephew. "Everything good? You look...off."

Everything was most certainly *not* good.

Particularly with Tim trapped in some sort of silence hell.

Takes a woman.

Every time.

Fighting the tightness between her shoulders, Lucie lifted her chin and faced Henry and Mattie. "We, um, had a bit of an issue."

Mattie's blue eyes popped wide and ping-ponged from Tim to Lucie, Tim to Lucie.

"What issue? What happened?"

Lucie held up her hands. "Everything is fine now, but it was a little scary at the time."

Beside her, Tim hadn't moved. An absolute statue. Excellent. The always in charge detective had turned mute.

Well, she'd do this for him because she loved him, but he'd owe her. Big time.

"Okay, let's sit down for a few minutes and we'll explain."

Lucie gestured to the seats, and Mattie and Uncle Henry settled on the sofa. Lucie and Tim took the adjacent armchairs. As soon as her butt hit the chair, Lucie launched into a synopsis of the failed abduction—leaving out the part about Tim snooping, obviously.

For a moment, Henry sat speechless. Absolutely dumbstruck. "Someone tried to kidnap you? In Paradise City? That never happens." He reached for Lucie's hands and squeezed. "I'm so sorry we put you in that position."

This poor man. Here he'd tried to help the woman he loved and wound up feeling guilt. How many times had Lucie been in that same position? Call her naive but doing the right thing shouldn't result in problems. "Oh, Uncle Henry, it's not your fault."

"What did the police say? Did they catch him?"

The previously mute-struck Tim cleared his throat and a smidge of relief loosened that pesky tension locked between Lucie's shoulder blades.

"Not yet," Tim said. "The plates on the SUV were stolen. It's not uncommon. Makes the vehicle harder to trace when they belong to someone else."

Mattie did that ping-pong thing with her gaze again. Lucie wanted to smack her. She looked like something out of a Frankenstein movie. A Mel Brooks' version.

Plus, she'd apparently gotten ensnared in Tim's trap of silence.

Accustomed to verbal swordplay while questioning witnesses, Tim leveled his detective stare on her. "What's really tripping me up is the guy mentioning Lucie's mom, considering they don't live here."

"Yes," Henry agreed. "That's odd. Did you ask your mother about that?"

Lucie nodded. "We did. The only Paul she knows is from our hometown."

Lucie met Mattie's gaze, then shut up. She couldn't do it.

Couldn't ask this woman, right in front of Henry, if she was a liar.

"What?" Mattie shot, her shoulders flying back. "Why are you looking at me like that?"

Tim held out a hand. "Don't get excited. We're putting pieces together and Lucie *was* walking Aphrodite."

Henry's head drooped forward. "You think this guy was after *Mattie*?"

"Not saying that, Unc. I'm a cop, I'm working through what we know."

Henry shook his head. "That's ridiculous. She doesn't even know a Paul." Henry swiveled to the still silent Mattie. "Honey, tell him."

Yes, honey, tell him.

The few seconds of quiet lingered, the stifling pressure filling the space like a flash flood. Just...*bam*. Mattie sagged back into the sofa and looked away, staring at the curtains covering the front windows. From their first meeting, there'd been a vitality about her. Whether a result of her sun-bronzed skin, the makeup she'd applied with expert care, or her giant hair, when Mattie arrived, everyone knew it. Somehow, in the last thirty seconds, all that energy vaporized.

Kinda like the time Lucie showed up for her dad's last trial and heard the guilty verdict. The power of her Notre Dame education couldn't overcome that particular area of Lucie's history. That one stayed with her.

It was one of the main reasons she avoided saying her last name when meeting people.

Crappy?

Yes.

In her defense, Lucie wasn't sure what to do about the

embarrassment that plagued her regarding her father's lifestyle.

And, now, looking at Mattie, she sensed something...familiar.

Something humiliating.

Moving on emotional instinct, Lucie rose from her spot and squatted in front of Mattie, gently touching her knee. "We're not accusing you of anything." *Not much anyway.* "We're trying to figure this out."

"Anyways," Henry shot, "this couldn't be about Mattie. You said the guy mentioned your mother. Mattie doesn't have any kids and her mother has been dead for years. Must have been mistaken identity."

"That could be," Tim said. "I'd like to hear it from Mattie, though."

The woman's face crumpled, an epic collapse. She pressed her eyes shut, scrunched her nose, and peeled her lips back.

What the heck?

As fast as the energy had left the room, it came roaring back. A rogue wave about to take out an entire village. A spurt of tears created black streaks below Mattie's eyes. She whipped her head toward the curtains again and swiped at the tears.

"I'm so sorry. I'm so sorry."

Lucie gave Tim the side eye, but he sat still, his mouth firmly closed. Figuring he knew better how these situations unfolded, she stayed quiet, not moving a muscle.

Uncle Henry leaned over, set his hand on Mattie's shoulder, and squeezed. "Honey?"

"Oh, Henry," Mattie wailed, swinging her arms up.

And, here we go...

"What is it, peaches?"

Peaches?

Tim gawked. His entire body seeming to fold in. An absolute jaw-dropping, shocked-the-hell-out-of-him response. Lucie bit her lip, fighting a laugh. Holy smokes, how inappropriate would that be right now?

Mattie threw herself into Henry's arms, her sobbing and shrieking enough to split Lucie's skull.

Tim rubbed both his hands over his face. "Okay," he said. "Let's calm down."

"Calm?" Henry asked, his voice laced with haughty indignance. "You got her all wound up."

"*Me?* What did I do? We were trying to help by walking the damned dog. Don't blame me for this shit-show."

"Aahhhh," Mattie wailed again.

"You stop screaming!" Henry said.

Huh. This thing had—to Lucie's sick satisfaction—gone totally Rizzo.

Finally. Tim's weak spot revealed. All these months he'd been damned near perfect. Normal family, friends, habits. Normal, normal, normal. On some level, it left her feeling subpar.

Now?

Not so much.

Lucie stuck her fingers in her mouth and let out an ear-shredding whistle. She didn't typically use the skill, but when she did, it got everyone's attention. Tim and Uncle Henry's heads snapped around, both falling silent, but Mattie? She might give Ro a run-off in the election for Drama Queen with that psychotic shrieking.

"All righty then," Lucie said. "I'm out."

Tim gave her his death glare.

"What? Usually the whistle works. I'm at a loss."

The doorbell rang. "Great." Tim flapped his arms. "The way she's screaming, that has to be the cops."

He marched to the door and swung it open. Roseanne, Joey, Mom, and Dad, all showered and looking spiffy, stood on the porch. A fresh wave of horror washed over Lucie.

The situation was looney enough without adding her crew to it.

But Tim waved them in. "How appropriate. Join the show."

Lucie burst out laughing. Poor Tim.

"For the love of God," Ro said to Mattie. "Quit that screaming. We heard you from the driveway."

No inquiry about why Mattie might be losing her mind. Just a command to cease. From the one who usually created the chaos.

Fascinating.

When Mattie didn't quiet down, Ro marched straight over, grabbed both of her arms, and shook her. *Oh, boy.*

"Sister! You're acting like a nut-job and giving me a headache. Believe me, whatever you're going through, I get it. Girls like us, we need the release, but enough already. Snap out of it and let us help you."

Mattie shut her mouth. That quick. Just...over.

"Thank you, sweet baby Jesus," Mom said.

Joey stuck a finger in his ear. "Are my ears bleeding? Dad, you see any blood?"

Dad snorted. "Henry, got any scotch?"

Henry wrapped his hand around his forehead and massaged. "Cabinet over the sink. Pour me one, too. Make it a double."

Tim made his way back to the seating area and met Lucie's eye. "Seriously, this is a nightmare."

She patted his arm. "Everyone take a seat and breathe. Please. Mattie, can I get you anything?"

A straitjacket perhaps?

"What I need you can't give me."

Ro squeezed next to Mattie and put an arm around her. "Don't be too hasty. Lucie is resourceful."

How sweet was she? Nutty as a fruitcake, as Mom would say, but truly one in a million.

Mattie shivered, her whole-body quaking as she wrapped her arms around her mid-section and rocked forward. "Oh, my God. It's happening."

"If she freaks out again," Ro said, "I'm slapping her."

Lucie squatted in front of Mattie once more and touched her knee. It worked the last time, might as well give it a go again. "Mattie, you're fine. Whatever is going on, we'll help you. Do you know who the man is that attacked me?"

Mattie shook her head.

"What about Paul?"

A long pause gave up the goods. Whatever this was, Mattie had information. Finally, she gave a slight nod.

Tim needed to handle this. Not only was Henry his family, but he was the detective and knew how to deal with these situations. She looked up at him, now standing beside the sofa. He jerked his chin enough for Lucie to know he wanted her to continue.

Great. *Thanks for that, fella.*

"It's all right." Lucie gave Mattie's arm a squeeze.

"It's *not*," Mattie said. "I put you in danger." She glanced around the room. "All of you."

"I don't understand," Henry said.

"Oh, Henry. I'm so sorry."

"For what?"

"Everything."

Dad entered the room carrying two rock glasses. Talk about a healthy two fingers of scotch. He handed one off to Henry who slammed it home and passed the empty glass back to Dad.

"Well—" Mom slapped her hands together, "—time to go."

Mattie shook her head. "No. You'll find out anyway and I'd prefer you hear it from me. I put your daughter in danger today. You deserve to know why."

Mom sat in one of the armchairs. "Whatever it is, I'm sure you didn't mean it."

That was Mom. Always the forgiving one. She'd have to be considering she hadn't divorced dad after all these years.

Henry met Mattie's eyes for a long second. Something crossed between them, the energy bringing a settled calm over the room. Lucie glanced at Tim, gave him a small smile. How many times had they exchanged a similar look? And how many had he been the steadying force in her storm?

Plenty. More than she could count.

And she loved him for it.

Apparently, that inner strength was a family trait because Henry, with just a glance, seemed to shore Mattie up.

"Tell me what's wrong," Henry said. "We'll fix it."

Mattie peered at the extra people before looking back at Henry. "I need to speak to you alone. You deserve to hear it first."

With that, leaving no room for argument, she popped out of her seat and headed for Henry's bedroom.

"Oh, we have to listen in," Ro said.

Ohmygod. "No! It's their business."

Tim headed for the kitchen. "I'm with Ro. It was theirs until you almost got abducted."

What in God's name was happening? Her straight-arrow boyfriend had turned into one of the crazies. "Has a zombie gotten to you? Sucked your brain out or something?"

"Maybe so. All I know is there's a vent in the kitchen. Might be able to hear from there."

Ro toddled after him on her mile-high sandals. "Ooh, O'Hottie. Always on the ball."

"That is *so* not right," Lucie said to Joey and Dad.

"Baby girl, you're preaching to the choir. I got locked up on a bum beef."

And here we go. Leave it to Dad to bring his own issues into this. Somehow everything always rolled back to Joe Rizzo. In his mind, the tax evasion was trumped up because the Feds couldn't nail him on organized crime charges.

"Right or not," Joey said, "I'm effing curious."

"Joey! Come on."

"Sorry, Luce. Dad, you coming?"

Dad shrugged. "Why not?"

Lucie stood in the living room, watching them all huddled, heads dipped, around the air conditioning vent in the kitchen. Unbelievable. When Mom joined them, Lucie shook her head.

"You guys are horrible people."

"You just figured that out?" This from Joey, the smartass.

Ro turned back and stuck her tongue out. "You know you want to. Just hop off that high-horse and get over here."

Tim swatted her hand. "Sssshhh."

"What is it? Something good?"

That fast, a switch in Lucie's brain flipped and she was in motion, heading straight for the kitchen vent. So much for respecting their privacy. "What did they say?"

Joey rolled his eyes. "If you'd shut up, we could hear."

"Swear to God," Tim said, "if you two start I'm throwing you both out."

Whoa. Mr. Always Collected getting his panties in a wad.

"Henry," Mattie's voice streamed through the vent, "I'm so sorry, but I haven't been honest with you."

"Holy cow," Lucie said. "This vent thing really works."

Tim held his finger to his lips. "*Ssshhh.* His bedroom is on the other side of this wall. It's the same duct. Which means, we have to whisper. If we can hear them—"

"We can hear you!"

That would be Henry. Screaming at them through the vent. "Get away from there before I put you all out on the curb."

Crud.

Tim shook his head. "Thanks, Rizzos."

Sufficiently chastised, they shuffled out of the kitchen and dropped into the living room chairs again. Ten minutes later, Henry and Mattie entered. Mattie's makeup appeared smudged, her eyes red and swollen, and the fat curls in her hair had flopped. She walked toward them, chin high, meeting everyone's gaze.

Henry's body language was all over the place. Tight jaw, hands loose at his sides, stride quiet.

After spending so much time with dogs, Lucie learned they had a gift, an ability to sense rotten energy. Right now she must have been channeling her dog instincts, because she wanted to run screaming from Henry. "I'm sorry we were eavesdropping."

Mattie waved it off. "You'll find out anyway, so—" she glanced at Henry, "—I'm going to tell you what I told Henry. After your ordeal, you deserve answers."

Tim rose from the armchair and waved Mattie to it. "Please. Sit."

She took him up on it and eased into the chair, smoothing her hands over her hair, then scanning each of their faces before finally settling on Lucie. "My father is in jail."

Heavy silence lingered for a few seconds until Ro snorted. "Oh, honey, that's not unusual with this bunch."

Mattie gave her a weak smile. Leave it to Ro.

Any other time, Lucie would laugh. This though? Twisted.

"He's seventy-four years old," Mattie said. "He's owned a real estate brokerage firm in Boston for the last thirty-five years. Eight months ago he was convicted on several charges involving real estate fraud."

The flyer she'd seen in Mattie's house was about a Boston condo complex. Perhaps a deal her father had brokered?

"I'm sorry," Lucie said.

Of all the people in the room, she knew the pain of a daughter—always daddy's little girl—watching her father go to a cage.

Mattie shrugged. "I'm getting used to it. It's taken me a while to adjust to the anger. I'm not sure I'll get over it, but I'm learning to live with it. Two years ago he made me a partner in the agency. He wanted to pass his legacy on to me."

"Uh-oh," Tim said.

No kidding. If Mattie was a partner in a business involved with fraud, she could be a co-conspirator.

Poor Henry. No wonder he looked like a bomb hit him.

Mattie lifted her chin again. "I know what you're thinking. I didn't know what my dad was doing. I trusted him. I never even worked on that account with him."

"All right," Tim said. "What does this have to do with what happened this morning?"

Mattie gazed up at Henry, who stared straight ahead. "I'm so sorry, Henry."

"Just tell them," he said.

After losing his wife, he'd fallen in love with a woman who'd duped him. To Henry, Mattie Mournay must be an illusion. Lucie found herself wildly impressed with Mattie's deception skills. With as much as Lucie and Tim shared, she'd never be able to keep up the charade.

"My father was arrested at our office. I had no idea what was going on. They took all of our files and computers. We were left with nothing. It was all evidence. I met later with Dad's lawyer, who walked me through the charges. Our largest client, That Girl."

Lucie cocked her head. "The doll place?"

"Yes."

That Girl was a modern-day phenomenon. Parents would send the company a photo of their child and for the measly sum of four hundred and ninety-five dollars have a doll—a twin—made. Once it arrived, the owners were free to bring the toy into the retail store and outfit it in any of the thousands of over-priced accessories.

In Lucie's mind, the whole thing was a tad creepy, but whatever.

"Big client," Joey said.

"Yes. We were responsible for locating retail properties for the entire northeast. They'd been with us fifteen years. Before the Landons even entered the picture, my father worked for That Girl."

"The Landons?"

"Geoffrey Landon." Mattie gritted her teeth. "That weasel. He was That Girl's in-house real estate person. A vice president, no less. They hired him a few years ago. Then his father, Paul, came into the picture."

The elusive Paul revealed. "Ah," Lucie said.

Mattie nodded. "I'm so sorry."

"It's all right. You didn't know." Lucie rolled her hand for Mattie to continue.

"Dad met Paul at a golf outing. One thing led to another and he arranged for Dad to meet with some big-time developers. That's all I knew. Then Dad was arrested for fraud."

Tim sat on the sofa arm. "What was the charge about?"

"Dad and Geoffrey were found guilty of taking bribes from developers."

Joey let out a whistle. "Good one."

Lucie smacked his arm. "Shut it."

"Don't start." Tim eyed them then went back to Mattie. "How did the bribery work?"

"The developers would give Dad and Geoffrey money, trips, or whatever. There's something about shell companies and Dad being a silent partner. I really don't know. It was all so upsetting."

What did any of this have to do with Lucie getting kidnapped?

"So, how did you get here?"

Tim, Mr. Mind Reader. He knew exactly how to keep things on course.

Mattie nodded. "As I said, I didn't know anything about the fraud. Nothing. Then one day I started getting threats. Strange men following me, a dead rat in my mailbox." She shuttered. "That was the worst. I went to visit my father and told him what was happening. He thought Paul Landon was behind it. Apparently, Paul's a bit shady. And since I was a partner in the agency, Dad said Paul probably thought I knew something that could get him convicted."

Tim shook his head, trying to keep it all straight. "Had Paul been arrested?"

"No. That was the problem. His son and my dad were arrested. The DA is Simon Torrance. He went to my dad and told him he couldn't make a case against Paul and that he'd have to testify against him. My dad wouldn't do it. Then they turned to me. Asking all sorts of questions about what I knew. Nobody seems to understand I wasn't involved."

Lucie blurted her first thought. "Did you get a lawyer?"

"Yes. That was the first thing I did. He told me to give him some time. He went to the prosecutor, but Simon Torrance is, well, aggressive. Always has to win. He told my attorney he could assemble a case against me. I knew he was bluffing because I hadn't done anything wrong. My lawyer said if Mr. Torrance had enough evidence, he'd have indicted me already. Basically, the DA was trying to bully me. My lawyer told me to sit tight and see what happened. Sit tight. While I have dead rats in my mailbox."

"You lammed it," Joey said.

"Does that mean I ran? Yes. I...lammed...it. I know that makes me look guilty, but I wanted the threats to stop. I have a daughter to protect and thought if I ran, Paul Landon would realize that I wanted no part of the fraud or Boston."

Her daughter. *Tell your mother Paul knows where she is.* That's what the attacker said.

"You don't have the accent," Tim added.

"I worked on it. Very hard. For the first month, I kept to myself and watched videos online of people from California. I copied their speech patterns."

"That was smart," Ro said.

"I *am* smart. Aside from trusting my father. I changed my name and started over. I even sent my daughter away. Her father left us when she was two. God knows where that loser is. Sending her away was the hardest part of all of this. I miss her so much, but it's not fair to her. To have to live off the grid like this. I want her to live a normal life. Well, as much as possible."

"It makes sense now," Lucie said.

Mattie cocked her head. "What?"

"Maybe the attacker thought I was your daughter."

"She's only seventeen."

"From a distance, Lucie looks young," Tim said. "And she was walking your dog."

"I've been so careful. You have no idea. Fake name and IDs. A new social security number. All of it so I could hide. And then, last night when I came home I found a flyer tucked under my door. I don't know what to do."

Lucie perked up. "What flyer?"

"It's an announcement. The grand opening of one of Paul Landon's condo buildings in Boston. He must have delivered it. I don't know how he found me. I did everything right."

Tim sat back, drummed his fingers on his thigh. "Well, Mattie, I'd say you missed something, because they *did* find you. And they think Lucie is your daughter."

EIGHT

"Excuse me."

Henry pushed off the sofa and marched straight to the kitchen. From Lucie's vantage point, she lost sight of him, but the hard close—not quite a slam—of the back door was a good indicator he needed air.

Or silence.

Possibly both.

Mattie blinked a few times, fighting her water works, then peered at the floor. "He's so angry with me."

"Can you blame him?"

Throughout all Lucie's oddball situations, the arguments they caused, the risks she'd taken with her own safety, Tim had handled all of it in a calm, assertive manner. Those incidents aside, she'd seen him interact countless times with idiot valets who lost his keys or customer service people who provided zero help. Even when infuriated, he'd never been cruel.

Until now.

"Whoa." She held up her hands. "Did you really just say that?"

Mattie wiped away a fresh batch of tears. "He's right. And, no, I can't. Henry doesn't even know my real name."

"What *is* your real name?"

This from Ro, who'd somehow managed to remain calm and not fly into one of her drama girl episodes. It wasn't every day this crew met someone with a more interesting past than Joe Rizzo.

Mattie's mouth tipped into a wistful smile. "Natalie. Natalie Berringer."

"We won't squeal," Dad said.

He gets her. Given his run-ins with the law, Dad shared the most in common with this woman. He understood the crushing emotional toll of criminal investigations and potential jail time.

Yes, most, if not all of it, was Dad's fault. He'd chosen his lifestyle. Mattie—Natalie, whatever her name was—suffered the humiliation of her father's actions. And Lucie knew all about that.

Tim sat back in his chair and ran both palms up his forehead. The good detective had a headache.

Lucie stood and patted his shoulder. She was ticked at him for being mean, but he didn't deserve a migraine. "I'll get you an ibuprofen."

"Thanks."

"They're in the drawer near the stove," Mattie said.

Lucie moved to the kitchen and spotted Henry standing in the yard, hands on his hips. She grabbed the medicine then opened the back door, sticking her head out.

"You okay?"

He laughed in that rueful way people do when the only other option is to cry. Or pummel something.

"Lucie," he said, "I have no idea what I am."

"Understandable. This is a lot. Even for me and that's

saying something. If you want to talk, I'm here. I've grown up around a criminal lifestyle. I understand the stress and chaos it creates."

"Are you defending her?"

"Not at all. I'm saying there's more to it than her lies. But you need time to process it. Give yourself that time. Just know that I'm here. I get it, Henry. More than you know."

She eased the door closed, grabbed Tim's abandoned water bottle from the table, and headed back to the living room, tossing the meds to him. He popped it open and dumped three in his hand.

Lucie snatched the bottle back and checked the dosage directions. "Tim, these are one tablet—"

"Yeah." He slammed all three at once and took a swig of water. "What's your point?"

My God. Now she'd have to watch and make sure he didn't overdose.

Across from Lucie, Ro clucked her tongue. "Well, it finally happened. O'Hottie has straight up lost his mind. We'll be pumping his stomach before this is over."

"No, we won't," Tim said. "What we are doing is calling the police."

Mattie's head swiveled around so fast it should have zipped right off her shoulders and taken flight. "I can't. I won't do it. I have a daughter to protect."

Tim softened his features, let some of his clenched jaw loosen. "I understand. But taking off won't help. They'll find you again. And again. And again. You'll live on the run. Is *that* fair to your daughter?"

Lucie shook her head. "Mattie, he's right. It has to be a horrible way to live. And what about Henry?"

At the mention of Henry, the room became quiet and Mattie's brows drew together, creasing the skin above her nose. She peered into the kitchen and Lucie sensed hope crashing. Twenty-four hours ago this woman was a vital, cheery—annoyingly so—creature. Now?

A pack of wolves might as well circle with the desperation wafting from her.

"He won't want me after this," Mattie said. "Tim's right, I can't blame him."

Oh, ouch. Lucie gave Tim the stink-eye. He propped his elbows on his knees and lopped his head forward. *Yeah, fella, you've got some 'splainin' to do.*

"Look," Tim said. "I apologize for what I said. We were in the heat of it and I lost my head. It's no excuse for crappy behavior. I'm sorry."

Mattie shrugged. "It's all right. You love your uncle. He's lucky that way. And, I know you're trying to help."

Fugitive or not, Mattie had a sweetness about her. No wonder Henry loved her.

"If you ask me," Lucie said, "we shouldn't get ahead of ourselves on this. The priority is Paul Landon. What does he think you know?"

"I have no idea. He probably assumes, since I was Dad's partner, I have evidence."

"Do you?"

"I don't think so. The police took everything from the office and my dad's home."

Joey held up a finger. "Yeah, but did they check the walls? Under the floors? Could be a gold mine."

Leave it to Joey. Lucie swore one day he'd take a sledgehammer to their family home.

After a long few seconds of Mattie pondering Joey's statement, she wrinkled her nose. Apparently, she didn't like the idea of demolishing a house either.

"Not that I know of," she said. "Everything was intact when I left. I closed it up myself."

Tim sat back, his big shoulders easing against the chair as he gnawed on his bottom lip. "Did your father give you any papers to hold?"

"No. Nothing." She paused. Opened her mouth, then closed it again. "Wait. I don't know if this will help, but when Dad made me a partner, he gave me copies of the partnership agreement. He insisted everything be legal in case anything happened to him."

"When was that?"

Mattie considered the question. "About two years ago. I don't remember the exact date. I'd have to look."

"And when did he start working with Paul Landon?"

Another pause. Lucie held her breath. That pause wasn't just pregnant, it was three weeks overdue. And she didn't need her master's degree to tell her Mattie might have become a partner in her father's company right around the time Landon showed up.

"Oh, my God," Mattie said.

Tim sat straight again, tapped his finger on the chair's arm. "Get me those papers."

"All I have are copies. They're at my house. Dad still has the originals. I think they're in a safe deposit box."

"That's fine. Let's get them. I'll talk to my uncle and see if he wants to come with us." Tim stood and faced the Rizzo crew. "I'll be right back. Why don't you all head to your place and relax?"

"Good idea," Lucie said. "Do you want me to go with them?"

"No. If it's all right with Mattie, I'd like you to review the paperwork." He faced Mattie. "Lucie has an investment banking background. She's also a hell of a business woman."

Aww, my man. So hot.

Mattie nodded. "Of course. I'll do anything."

"I'm hungry," Joey said. "Let's go eat."

"We just had lunch," Ro said.

"That was two hours ago. You want I should starve? We'll go to the pool bar. Dad, Ma, let's go. Happy hour."

"Ooh, good." Mom held up her hands. "I like the rum punches that bartender makes."

"Enjoy," Lucie said as they all filed out.

With Tim outside with Henry and everyone else gone, Lucie turned to Mattie still sitting in the chair, her body slumped back.

Deflated.

As a rule, Lucie had learned not to trust new people. Something her parents, due to Dad's illicit activities, had jammed into her psyche from childhood. They never knew who might try to infiltrate Dad's crime boss world. Paranoia ran high regarding federal agents and assassins alike. It wasn't a good way to live, and her parents had cut her off from making new friends as a result.

Without question, Lucie knew her father's protective instincts were meant to keep her safe. His life choices may have been a disaster, but when it came to intentionally bringing Lucie into his criminal world? Never.

Dad simply wouldn't do it.

But Mattie's father had, and Lucie couldn't imagine how deep *that* betrayal cut.

She wandered over and rested one hip on the chair while slipping an arm over Mattie's shoulder. "I'm sorry this is happening to you. My dad is..."

She stared at the front door her father just walked

through. Complicated man. Maddening man. *Focus, Luce.* She had time to deal with her feelings about Dad later.

For now, she'd concentrate on Mattie. "I'm sure you've heard stories about him. He's not perfect. I've spent years overcoming the mob princess label. As frustrated and angry as I was with him, I knew he'd never cross certain lines." She shook her head. "I can't imagine the heartbreak of a father bringing his innocent daughter into criminal activity. I'm so sorry."

"I'm madder at myself. How could I have been so stupid?"

"For trusting your father? How is that your fault? You were business partners. When you trust someone, your heart gets in the way. Don't beat yourself up. Believe me, it won't help. Let's figure out how to get you out of this. Then you can worry about what your father did."

The back door thumped and, a second later, Tim stepped into the living room, his all-serious cop face intact. Henry lagged behind, all sunken cheeks and misery.

Heartbreak all around today.

Tim smacked his hands together and the sharp clap charged the air. "Let's go. Henry and Mattie can talk while Lucie and I read over the papers."

Lucie's hot Irish detective was in get-it-done mode. Fine. The quicker they figured this out, the quicker they could get back to a drama free vacation.

TIM AND LUCIE sat on Mattie's patio, the late afternoon sun throwing shadows under the awning. Inside, Henry and Mattie discussed the state of their relationship. Lucie didn't envy either of them. In one day, everything they knew had shattered. How did two people claw their way back from that?

She glanced at Tim as he unclasped a manila envelope Mattie had given him. As much as she loved him, could she move beyond a deception that intense?

Who knew? She certainly hoped to never find out.

"Incorporation papers," Tim said, sliding the documents between them.

She scooted closer to him, so she could read. "Let me go through them one time."

"Go ahead. Sorry to drag you into this. Not exactly the visit we wanted."

Waving it off, she picked up the papers. "Henry is family. Once we get this squared away, we'll go back to our vacation. Plus, I kinda feel sorry for them."

"Yeah. My uncle is devastated. He loves her." Tim jammed both palms into his eye sockets. "My mom will shit herself."

"Maybe. But she's not here, so let's focus on what we can do now. Give me time to read this and we'll come up with a plan."

Minutes later, Mattie and Henry joined them at the patio table.

"I just read the paperwork," Lucie said.

Henry still wore the drained, pale-faced look of a man in shock, but at least he'd hung around to offer support.

Poor man. The woman he loved was an imposter.

"Did you find anything?" Henry asked.

"Yes and no. Mattie, what was the name of your realty firm?"

"Island Management. Why?"

Lucie shuffled through the documents. "Okay. I see

those here. But there's another set of papers." She handed the stack over. "Island Investments?"

Mattie shook her head. "I have no idea."

Not the answer Lucie wanted—or expected. *Yeesh.* She shuffled through the pages, got to the Island Investments paperwork, and—*pfft, pfft, pfft*—shuffled some more to the end. She set a page in front of Mattie. "Your signature is on them. Dated the same day as the Island Management pages. Island Investments is a Wyoming LLC though."

Tim gave her the cop face. "Wyoming? What's that about?"

"It's actually not uncommon. Wyoming is friendly to shell companies. The bankers in my old office called it the offshore of the American prairie. Laws there protect the privacy of business owners."

"Meaning," Tim said, "it's a hot bed for millionaires hiding their money or potential criminal behavior."

"It can be. Yes. Not everyone who forms a shell company is a criminal, though. Some might just want to protect their privacy, so they file in Wyoming."

Mattie scanned the document then looked at Henry for a brief second before meeting Lucie's gaze. Beyond the patio, a couple birds tweeted at each other. Lucie tore her gaze from Mattie's, giving her a second to get her thoughts together.

Mattie, too, stared out at them. "They do that every afternoon. At first it annoyed me. Now it feels like home." She blew air between her lips then held up the papers. "I have no idea what Island Investments is. My father brought me a stack and told me to sign them."

Leaning in, Tim held his hand out and Mattie passed the pages over. He flipped through the stack, perusing each one. "When you signed, did you read the whole thing?"

"Yes. Every page. I don't remember seeing the Island Investments agreement. Wait. Oh, he didn't…"

She set the Island Management document on the table and stacked the Island Investments one on top, lining the signatures up one above the other. "Oh, my God. That son of a bitch. I can't believe it."

Whoa. "What?"

She jabbed her finger against the documents. "I shouldn't admit this. I feel like a fool."

"Don't," Tim said. "You'd be shocked at who gets swindled. I'm talking top businesspeople. It happens every day. Tell us what you're thinking so we can help you."

"My father and I had a system. If documents needed to be signed and one of us wasn't available, we signed the other's name."

"You forged his signature."

Mattie winced. "It sounds horrible, but yes. We only did it on routine stuff."

Forgery was routine? Though with Lucie's family history, definitely not her place to judge.

"You know," Mattie circled one hand, "checks to pay bills or commissions. Things that kept our business running."

Tim leaned in on his elbows. "You're saying your father signed the Island Investments incorporation papers on your behalf?"

"No. He forged my signature." She pointed on the Island Investments document. "See this swoop at the bottom of the N? It's different than my actual signature. Close, but not as pronounced. That's my father's version."

Tim took a minute to analyze the documents then sat back, his direct gaze locked on Mattie. "Your father formed a corporation without your knowledge."

"It appears so."

Wowie, wow, wow. And Lucie had issues with her Dad? Holy smokes, if Mattie's father did that, what else had he done? Lucie waggled her fingers and Tim handed her the document. "The registered agent on this corporation is listed as Helen Craft. Who is she?"

Mattie blinked. "Registered agent?"

"Yes. When you form a company in a different state, there's a third party responsible for handling paperwork. It's usually tax forms, correspondence from the Secretary of State. Lawsuits. In this case, the registered agent is Helen Craft."

"I don't know her."

Tim drummed his hand on the table. "We need to find her."

In complete agreement, Lucie nodded. "During my banking days, there was always talk about clients and shell companies. Shells made it easy for investors to move money around and avoid the IRS. Maybe Helen Craft is a registered agent for other corporations. If so, the good news is, Wyoming requires all agents to live within the state."

Tim lifted one hip and dug his phone from the back pocket of his shorts. "Ladies, let's find Helen Craft."

WHILE TIM BUSIED himself making calls, Lucie borrowed Aphrodite for some neighborhood reconnaissance. She summoned Ro for protection—in case the kidnapper made a second attempt. In a normal world, one would use the pit bull. In Lucie's? The better bet would be Ro.

Lucie stood on Mattie's front lawn with Uncle Henry keeping watch from the porch. The Escalade golf cart rounded the corner, its engine's whir rising with increased speed. Now in full view, Ro sat behind the wheel, her long sable hair blowing straight back as she hit the gas, one fist pounding the air.

Complete maniac.

Her BFF skidded to a stop at the curb, her lips wide with a toothy smile. She wore a tailored button-down blouse —*that might come in handy*—and a denim mini skirt with a pair of spiked-heeled strappy sandals that wrapped around her ankles. As usual, Ro put the *va* in va-va-voom.

"Oooh-wee!" She banged her palm against the steering wheel. "I love this thing, Luce. Wicked fun."

"I see that. You need to be careful."

Using both hands, Ro flipped her hair back. "Don't be a downer." She fixed her brown eyes on Aphrodite. "Why are you walking her? You're on vacation."

Ha. Some vacation so far. "I'm not. Well, I am, but it's an undercover mission."

Four, three, two, one.

Ro tipped her chin down and peered at Lucie like she did when she wore her sexy-librarian reading glasses. "Don't tease me, Luce."

Unlike the majority of Lucie's inner circle, Ro was a sucker for Lucie's investigations. She liked the adventure. In a twisted way, so did Lucie. Unfortunately, they hadn't figured out how to flip the switch on their impulse controls and often wound up putting themselves in dangerous situations. They went all in. Every time.

Drove Tim nuts.

Oh.

Well.

Lucie laughed. "I'm not teasing you. Tim got a call from the cop who responded to my...uh...*incident* earlier."

No sense in calling it what it was, since they both knew Lucie almost went to sleep with the fishes.

Ro gave her an oh-really look. "Sister, if you're waiting for me to beg for details, forget it. Do tell."

"The cops canvassed the neighborhood and found a witness who spotted the SUV screaming down the street. It had a car rental company's logo on the corner of the windshield. Elite Rental by the airport."

"A *rental*. Fascinating."

Not really, but whatever. "There's a satellite office five miles from here. Thought we'd swing by and see what's what."

"Ha! I knew there was a reason I wore a button-down. I swear I'm psychic." She patted the seat beside her. "Hop in."

When Lucie didn't move, Ro made snoring noises.

"Sometime today, Luce, before Joey starts calling and asking questions. If we time this right, we'll be back before he gets suspicious. Now get in."

"I was thinking we could take a car."

Ro waved that off. "This thing has speed. And Joey just filled the tank. We can go two hundred and fifty miles on six gallons. How crazy is that?"

Still not convinced it was a wise move, Lucie loaded Aphrodite into the rear then slid in beside her. Some things simply weren't worth arguing over. Particularly with Ro.

"I'll sit back here," Lucie said. "The way you drive, no telling what might happen."

"Hold on, sister."

Vroom. She hit the gas, jerking Lucie's head back far enough to slip a disc. Aphrodite though was all over it, tipping her snout up into the breeze. She barked once then again as Ro sped down the street.

Lucie wrapped an arm around Aphrodite and nudged her closer. "I've got you. I won't let crazy driver lady hurt you."

"Oh, blah, blah. Keep it up and I'll take this next turn on two wheels."

She'd do it too. Still, Lucie held on to the dog. Why take chances? "*Anyway*, the cop who called Tim wouldn't give him the name of the renter."

"You're thinking we can get it out of them?"

"Yep. And, I won't lie, I was somewhat relieved when I saw you in a button-down shirt."

Ro laughed. Aside from being gorgeous, her knockers drew attention. Once she popped a button or two men dropped. *Boom.* Complete domination.

For years, Ro had been using her ample cleavage to score good seats at shows, extra discounts at retail stores, a free upsize at coffee shops, free oil changes. Whatever.

Joey didn't like her using her rack as a negotiating tool, but as big and mean as he could be, Ro wasn't afraid of him. When it came to her? He turned soft. The Joey version of soft anyway.

Ro hooked a left onto Paradise Way, the community's main drag, and maneuvered to the far right lane. The golf cart lane. To their left, the square bustled with people shopping in the boutiques and home decor businesses that lined the next two blocks. Ro honked at a sidewalk cafe jammed with folks, sending a blast of *O Sole Mio* to the diners.

"Helloooo," she called as they cruised by.

Lucie closed her eyes and prayed the ground might swallow her up. When nothing happened, she opened her eyes again.

Yep. Still here.

Minutes later, Ro made a right turn, honked at more pedestrians, one of whom jostled his coffee enough that it spurted onto his white shirt. The man waved a fist.

"Whoopsie." Ro said. "Just trying to be friendly."

"Maybe skip the honking. Why call any more attention to ourselves?"

"Be that way. Besides, we're pulling onto a four lane road and I need to focus."

"Just stay in the golf cart lane. Everyone will drive around you."

They rode in blessed silence while cars whooshed around them. Oddly, Lucie didn't mind cruising along in the cart. Uncle Henry's car would have been faster, but the warm sun and cool breeze, after a harsh Chicago winter, knocked the edge from Lucie's nerves.

Minutes later, Ro turned into a parking lot hosting a row of shiny cars. All high-end. Overhead, a large white sign with elegant lettering indicated they'd reached Elite Rentals.

"We made it alive," Lucie said.

"Har, har, smartass." Ro twisted around to face Lucie. "This is taking too long. Joey'll start calling any time now. And I'm not dealing with that. How are we playing this?"

"Let's go with Aphrodite first. We'll see if they have a bowl, so we can give her water."

"Luce, there's about five hundred markets along this road. That's the worst excuse ever." Ro pointed at the leash in Lucie's hand. "We'll tell them we returned a vehicle, but her leash must be under the seat. And it's her favorite."

"How is that gonna get us a name?"

Ro threw her arms up as she slid from the seat. "I have no idea. All I know is your pain in the ass brother is about to start blowing up my phone and then I'll have to kill him. Which, I don't want to do. Your mom will never forgive me." She turned back and grabbed her purse from the seat. "Let's go in and see what we have. If we need to, we'll slip someone a hundred bucks for giving us a name."

Ew. That was so…slimy.

Ro stared at her, waiting for a comment. She wouldn't get one. Right now, all Lucie wanted was to salvage this vacation. So if it took slime to get things on track, or Ro popping a few buttons, she was all for it.

Ready for the adventure, Aphrodite hopped out and followed Ro, who opened the building's door. The hanging bells swung then crashed back against it, filling the quiet space with a loud *brrrrnnnggg*. Aphrodite leaped and swatted at the strap.

"Great," Ro muttered. "She thinks it's a toy."

"Off," Lucie said, her voice an octave lower.

Aphrodite clamped onto the bells and tugged. So much for the I'm-in-charge voice.

Lucie bent low to pry them from Aphrodite's jaws. Holy cow, she had a lock on them.

"Ma'am, no dogs allowed."

Before turning her attention from Aphrodite, Lucie pasted a smile on and faced the middle-aged and extremely blonde woman behind the counter. Yikes, that yellow shade could light up a city.

"I'm…uh." She tugged on the bells again. "Sorry. She thinks it's a toy."

"I see that. Please take her outside."

As if Lucie wasn't trying? Finally, she dropped to her knees to survey the situation. One bell in the mouth and the strap sticking out both sides. This could be a problem.

"We need a treat."

Ro sighed. "Oh. My God. My work is seriously never done." She set her purse on the chair next to Lucie and pulled a five from her wallet before facing the blonde. "I'm soooo sorry about this. Do you have a vending machine? Maybe I can get a treat there."

The woman grimaced. "It's an employee-only machine. You can't go back there."

Ro gave Lucie a look. "It seems we can't do a lot of things around here. So much for customer service."

"It's regulation," the woman said.

"All right. Well, we *wouldn't* want to get you *fired*. How about I give you money and you can buy me pretzels? Anything but chocolate. Chocolate can kill a dog—and we definitely don't want *that* happening in your fine establishment." Ro batted her eyes. "Do we?"

The shift to bitch-mode came early in this mission.

The blonde harrumphed. If this woman knew Ro at all, she'd know antagonizing her might earn a butt-whupping. Just ask Tiffy Nelson. To this day Tiffy crossed to the other side of the street when she walked past Coco Barknell.

The guys down at Petey's called it the Ro Effect.

Ro restrained herself but glared at the clerk. "Is there a manager here? Maybe they'll be more accommodating."

"Why do you need a manager?"

Ro smacked a bill on the counter. "We have a problem here. You want the dog gone and I'm trying to get us there. So either you're going back there and getting me pretzels or I am. Got it? You know what? Forget it. I'll call corporate and lodge a complaint." She rummaged in her Gucci purse, dug her phone out, and tapped the screen. "I'll just look up the number."

Biting her lip to hide a smile, Lucie stared down at Aphrodite still locked onto those damned bells.

The clerk snatched the bill off the counter. "Jake! I need help out here."

A second later, a guy in his early twenties appeared in the doorway. *This just got a whole lot better.* Ro gave him her back. Smug grin in place, she popped two buttons that revealed the edge of a sheer beige bra.

A two-button mission. *Look out, kid.* If he stared too long, he'd be lost forever.

The woman disappeared, and Jake stepped behind the counter. "Can I help you?"

"You sure can, honey," Ro said, leaning in enough to reveal a half-mountain of boobs. "Do those video cameras record audio?"

Jake's eyes zoomed right where Ro had intended. "Um... wow. No. Just video."

Once again, Ro smiled, and Lucie knew exactly where this was going. She gave up on Aphrodite and the bells and reached for Ro's purse, snatching a hundo—as Joey would say—from the wallet.

Time to double-down. Lucie smacked the hundred on the counter. "Perfect because we're about to bribe you."

The kid's head lopped forward. "What?"

Lucie tap-tap-tapped the bill. "Focus here. Some goon rented a black SUV from this agency and tried to kidnap me this morning."

The kid's gaze shot from Lucie to the bill. "No way."

"Yes, way." Ro brought his attention back to her cleavage. "Before Nurse Ratchet comes back, we'll give you this hundred bucks if you'll do your thing on your computer and give me a name. If he'd gotten my little Lucie into that car, no telling what he'd have done."

"Yes," Lucie added. "Do you really want some maniac running around in one of your vehicles abducting people? He could have killed me and dumped my body. He's a menace. How's that going to look for Elite Rental? I mean, renting cars to murderers. Really?"

The kid eyed the bill on the counter then went back to

Ro's cleavage. Not even bothering to hide it, she popped a third button.

Joey would have a fit.

"Two hundred bucks," the kid said.

Ro shook her head. "Apparently, I'm losing my touch. Fine. But you're giving me the name first. We're looking for a black SUV. A Lincoln, we think."

Lucie thought back to Mattie receiving the flyer after Tiki Night. Boston condo complex. Which could mean the person who left it flew in from there. "It may have been rented from the airport in the last few days."

The door leading to the rear of the building opened. *Uh-oh.* Ro snatched the bill on the counter, folding it in her hand.

"They had cheese crackers," the blonde announced as she plowed through the door.

Dammit.

"Excellent." Ro chirped. "She loves cheese."

When Ro didn't move from her spot, Lucie held up a hand. "I'll take those."

Behind the woman's back, Ro grabbed a brochure and jotted a quick note, handing it to the male clerk.

Lucie opened the package, and, at the first whiff of cheese, Aphrodite dropped the bells, sending them clanging against the door.

"Stay," Lucie said.

When the dog remained sitting—*good girl!*—Lucie slid her the cracker, almost losing half her hand in the process.

"All right," Ro said. "I think we're done here. Thank you for your help. Both of you."

The blonde cocked her head. "What *did* you come in for?"

"Oh," Lucie said, "forget it. We thought we left a leash in

a vehicle, but we didn't." She held up her phone. "My boyfriend found it."

Ro shoved her out the door and they hustled to the golf cart. Anticipating the ride, Aphrodite fired off a triple bark.

"*Sssh*," Ro said. "We'll go in a minute. I wrote him a note. Told him to get the name and meet us at the corner of the lot."

"You think he'll do it?"

"For that look at my tits plus two hundred bucks? He'd better."

NINE

After depositing Aphrodite at home, Lucie had Ro drop her off at Uncle Henry's before she went to meet Joey and his impending questioning. As issues went, Lucie got the better end of the deal by not having to put up with her PITA of a brother.

Tummy rumbling, Lucie marched inside and found Tim at the kitchen table, arms crossed and staring at his phone. Lord, had he been there this whole time?

At this point, she suspected dinner at Uncle Henry's favorite restaurant would be cancelled. But, cripes, they needed to eat.

She gave Tim a gentle smack on the shoulder then bent low for a smooch. Nothing too intense, just a quick peck she found an easy comfort in.

"It's after six o'clock. Please tell me you haven't been in this spot since I left."

"I've been in this spot since you left. I'm trying to find out who rented that damned car. If we were in Chicago, I'd have it by now. Here? Nobody gives a shit."

"I don't think that's necessarily true."

This had more to do with Tim not being able to get a job done. Her man liked being the resident Mr. Fix-It and this situation put him out of his jurisdiction. In a big way.

Tim grumbled something then tapped his phone. "Nothing."

"So, you're just sitting here, waiting for people to get back to you. Do you realize how crazy that is?"

"Pretty much, yeah. I need this guy's name."

"Sonny Peppers."

He finally dragged his gaze from his phone, snapping his head sideways and facing her. "Come again?"

"That's his name. We think. One Sonny Peppers from Boston rented a black Lincoln Navigator the day before yesterday. The only Navigator rented in the last two days."

"Are you messing with me?"

"No."

"Taunting me in some way?"

Unbelievable. "*No.* Sonny Peppers. That's who we're looking for."

"How do you know this?" He shifted his body sideways on the chair. "Is it going to piss me off?"

Tim didn't like Lucie getting into what he called 'screwball investigations.' Being law enforcement, of course he thought she should leave it to the police. But she, as a private citizen, wasn't bound by a constricting thing called the law. She didn't need warrants or probable cause to snoop around. Sure, Lucie might wind up in a cell, but a girl had to do what a girl had to do.

"Don't be mad," she said.

He closed his eyes. His lips moved but nothing came out. Prayer? Meditation? Anything was possible.

"Crap," he said. "What'd you do? I thought you were walking the dog."

Lucie dragged the chair beside Tim's out and dropped into it. "I was. Well, we were."

"Who's we?"

"Ro and I."

"Crap."

Lucie snorted and patted him on the shoulder again. "You're so paranoid. It's fine."

"Right. Please. One thing I know about you lunatics is that it's rarely fine. What did you do? And will I have to explain it to the local cops?"

Hopefully not. "Nope. All good."

I think.

How much jail time could someone get for bribing a car rental agency employee?

"What does *that* mean?"

"The guy took the money so I'm pretty sure he won't squeal."

Tim's jaw dropped. "He. Took. The *money*? What the hell did you do?"

Ho-kay. In a rare occurrence, the hot Irish detective got a little loud. O'Hottie might truly be going over the edge.

Lucie put up two hands. "Whoa, fella. I saw you getting stressed out—"

"Don't put this on me."

"I'm not. I'm just saying. I don't like you that way, so we went to the car rental place." She rolled her hand. "You know, to check it out. There's a satellite location a few miles from here. We got there, and Ro popped a few buttons. When that failed, we went for plan B."

"Extortion."

Oh, my God. Did he have to be so dramatic? "I wouldn't call it *that*. Motivation maybe."

Tim laughed, but it in no way resembled his authentic

belly laugh. This was more of a check-me-into-the-psych-ward maniacal giggle. "Justify it any way you want, Luce. It's extortion."

"Sonny Peppers, Tim. That's the guy's name. The name you've been sitting at this table trying to pry out of the local police. So lecture me all you want, but we have what you need."

For a few seconds, he simply stared at her until the hum of the refrigerator and the kerplunk of the ice maker dropping a fresh batch broke the spell. Slumped-shouldered, he tipped his head to the ceiling and mumbled. Something about God saving him.

Whatever. As much as she understood his frustration with her antics, the fact that he couldn't appreciate what she'd done irked her. She drummed her fingers on the table, reminding herself that Tim had always been patient with her when she'd gone rogue. "I know I make you crazy sometimes."

He gave up on praying and met her gaze. "I worry about you."

"We were fine. We had a giant pit bull with us."

"The one who ran when you almost got kidnapped."

"Well, that could've been an isolated incident. I also had Ro with me. And, you know that's nothing to sneeze at." She leaned in and touched her forehead to his. "We weren't in danger. I promise."

Either the lecture would last the next fifteen minutes, or he'd realize, finally, that nagging failed to stop her. Lucie dreaded moments like these. Despite knowing, without question, that Tim loved her, absolutely adored her, her chaotic life and her need to right a wrong, caused tiny fractures in their relationship.

Still, no matter his warnings, she simply could not stand

by and let a crime be committed. Particularly if it involved her family. One that now included Tim—and his relatives.

Family. The most important thing.

"Tim O'Brien, I love you. And if someone you love is in crisis, I'll do whatever I can to help."

"Even when it gives me hives."

She pulled back, shaking her head. "It doesn't. Maybe a headache, but not hives."

"Sonny Peppers," he said.

"Sonny Peppers."

"Did you happen to get an address?"

Now they were talking. "The Lafayette Motel. Room 225. It's not far from here."

"All right." He let out one of his long sighs then set his hands on the table and pushed out of his chair. "We'll check it out. With luck, we'll see the vehicle. Or Mr. Peppers."

Whoot! A stakeout with Tim. Great fun. "Shall we bring Ro's boobs?"

"Uh, no." He paused, ran a hand over his face and then dropped it to his side again. "Ah, hell, let's not rule it out completely."

"You gotta be kidding me."

Tucked under a White Sox baseball cap to hide his hair, Tim sat behind the wheel of his uncle's Lexus, staring into the rearview mirror with his jaw locked so tight it might fracture.

Afraid to turn and look at what had grabbed Tim's attention, Lucie refused to move. Two hours had passed while they sat in the darkening parking lot of the Lafayette Motel, one of those old-time deals with room doors facing out so everyone and their grandmother could see the comings and goings. An obvious fresh coat of peach stucco allowed the owners to post signs proclaiming, "Newly Remodeled!"

"What is it?"

Tim peeled his gaze from the mirror. "Your family just pulled in. In the damned golf cart that might as well be a neon sign. How the hell far can that thing go on a tank of gas?"

"When full, it'll go two hundred and fifty miles."

Abandoning her fear, Lucie spun around for a look. Yep. There they were. Joey and Ro in the front seat and Mom and Dad in the rear. This time her brother was behind the wheel.

Tim ran both hands over his face and sighed. "This is a nightmare."

"Let me talk to them."

Before she reached the door handle, he grabbed hold of her wrist. "We're supposed to be on a stakeout. Laying low to see if this guy shows up. Now you're gonna go out there and talk to those maniacs in the tricked-out golf cart that was on scene when he tried to snatch you? If he spots you, we're screwed."

The good detective had a point. *Hmm...* She snapped her fingers. "Give me your hat."

He cocked his head. Oh, she knew that look. Clearly her man was about to launch into questions she didn't want to waste time answering. Before he could respond, she plucked the ball cap from his head and flipped it on hers. It wobbled and fell to her eyebrows. Who knew he had such a giant cranium? But given the urgency of the golf cart blowing their cover, it would have to do.

"You're not—"

She opened the car door and bolted. No sense waiting around for the lecture.

Lucie marched toward the still moving Escalade, waited for Joey to come to a stop, and then squeezed onto the front seat, shoving Ro closer to the middle.

"Hey," her BFF said, "watch the skirt."

Forget the skirt. They had bigger problems. "Keep driving before Tim has a heart attack. What are you guys *doing*? We're trying to be inconspicuous and you pull up in this thing? After the guy saw it today?"

Because, really, how many custom-made Escalade knockoff golf carts could there be in Florida?

"Relax," Joey said. "Your guy is in a bar down the street."

"How do you know?"

"I tracked his cell phone," Dad said.

What? Lucie spun back to her father, looking mighty dapper in a golf shirt and cotton shorts. "What now?"

Dad waggled a hand. "After your sidekick here sang like a bird about you wacky broads going to the car rental place, I made calls. The dumbass rented the car in his real name. One of my guys in the PD was able to run his cell phone down."

Joey held up his phone. "I downloaded a spying app, so we can track him."

That had to be illegal. Didn't it?

Cripes. She reached across Ro and grabbed the phone. "He's in a bar?"

"Yeah. Irish pub. Two minutes from here."

She focused on the tiny blinking dot on Joey's screen. "And you're sure this is him?"

Affronted by her lack of faith, Dad grunted. "Who the hell else would it be?"

With this crew, it could be any number of innocent people.

"I think we should search his motel room." This from Ro

just as Joey cruised by Tim, still sitting in the dark in Henry's car. "Ooh." She lifted a hand. "There's O'Hottie. Woohoo!"

Oh. My. God.

Lucie latched onto Ro's hand and yanked it down. "Uh, stakeout. He's trying to lay low. And we're not searching anyone's room. I'm not up for a B&E tonight."

"No one said we had to break in."

This should be good. She gave Ro her smug face. "I can't wait to hear this. Joey, keep driving. Go around the block or something."

Joey pulled out of the parking lot, turned way too wide, and received a horn blast along with a stream of swear words that would make any military guy blush.

Shaking her head, Ro smacked Joey on his arm. "Precious cargo here. Watch it. Luce, you need to open your mind. All we need is a diversion. A fire!"

"A *fire*?" they all asked in unison.

"Of course. If there's one in his room, they have to break in and make sure nobody is passed out."

As much as Lucie wanted to protest, her goofy friend might have something there. A look inside Sonny Peppers' room might uncover who hired him.

"I'm not becoming an arsonist, but I like your thinking as far as an urgent situation. One of us goes running into the office yelling that Sonny won't answer his door. It's an emergency. And we need to get in there. The clerk opens the door and we're in."

At the corner, Joey got his act together and made a much neater right turn. "Except, the clerk isn't about to leave you in that room alone. And what if this mope comes back?"

Lucie held the phone up. "We'll know by the app."

Dad snapped his fingers. "Once we're in, I'll take care of it."

Said the parolee. Lucie whipped around. "Dad! You're on parole. You shouldn't even be involved."

"She's right, Joe," Mom said. "If you get arrested, I'm leaving you locked up. I've had it with that nonsense."

Joey snorted. "Good one, Ma."

Even for the Rizzos, this was an epic level of crazy. Thank God Tim missed it all.

Dad threw his hands up. "Jesus Christmas, all of you shut it. I go away for a couple years and suddenly I can't control my own family?"

Pretty much, yeah.

"Sorry, Dad," Joey, the suck-up, said.

"You keep driving and everyone listen. When the clerk leaves the room, someone distract him, and I'll jam the door so it doesn't close all the way."

Ro's hand shot up. "Me, me, me. I'll be the distractor. I'm good at that."

"You're not unbuttoning your shirt." Joey poked his finger at her. "Enough with that already."

"Son, you think this is James Bond or what? All she has to do is stand by the stairs and holler at the kid. As soon as he turns around, I'll jam the door. A few seconds and we're done."

For the first time, Lucie had to stand by and not only listen to her dad calmly devise a plan for an illegal search, but actually witness it. It should have sickened her.

"I like it," she said.

Right now, all she wanted was to help Uncle Henry. And Mattie. *Natalie.* Whatever her name was.

Lucie met Dad's eye. "Let's do this. I'll be the panicked girlfriend. All we have to do is convince Tim."

. . .

To his credit, Tim listened quietly while Lucie outlined their plan. To minimize interruptions, she'd dispatched the crazies to circle the block again, giving her time alone with Tim in the safety of Uncle Henry's car.

"No," he said. "I'm not having you in the middle of it if this guy comes back. I'll do it."

"You? How?"

"I'll say he's my brother."

Speaking of, Joey had apparently grown tired of circling and pulled up next to the driver's side door. Ro leaned over and knocked on the window.

Exasperated, Tim gave Lucie a hard stare. "Does she think I can't see them?"

He rolled the window down. "What's up?"

"We're ready," Ro said. "Let's do this."

"Joey, pull up. I can't get out of the damned car."

"Sorry, dude."

Joey hit the gas too hard and snapped all their heads backward.

"Joseph be careful! I'll have whiplash before this is over."

"Sorry, Ma."

Tim slid out, shutting the door behind him. "I'm going to the office. I'll tell the clerk Sonny is my brother."

Lucie hopped out and hustled around the front. "I'm going. If there's two of us, it'll be more distracting, so Dad can do his thing. We have to be careful with him."

As protective as Tim was, he had to see the logic in that.

"Fine." He started toward the office where a red Vacancy sign blinked. "I'm doing the talking though."

A minute later, they rushed inside where the rattle of a window unit air conditioner drowned out the tippety-tap of the clerk's fingers against the desktop computer's keyboard. The clerk jumped back, putting his hands up. "Don't shoot! There's no money."

What. The hell?

"I swear," the clerk pleaded. "They picked it up two hours ago."

"He thinks we're robbing him," Lucie said.

Not two minutes into this thing and she'd already blown the mandate to let Tim do the talking.

Tim turned to her. "Ya think?" He went back to the clerk. "Do you see a gun? Forget that. My brother is in room 225. He's not answering. He's been depressed lately, and I need to get in there. Give me the key. Sonny Peppers. 225."

"Please," Lucie said. "*Hurry.* He's not answering his phone either."

Apparently satisfied Bonnie and Clyde hadn't busted in on him, the clerk turned to the pegboard where plastic key rings holding actual keys hung. "Are you sure he's in there?"

Go, Tim.

"He told us to meet him here. Look, dude, his wife just left him, and he's been batshit crazy."

The clerk lifted the key from its peg. "I can't give you the key, but I'll check on him. You'll have to wait here."

Uh-oh. Talk about spoiling the plan.

Tim set both hands on the counter and leaned in, his big body looming over the scrawny clerk. "Either you're giving me that key, so I can check on my brother, or I'm kicking the door in. Got it?"

To add a little urgency, Lucie pulled her phone out. "Forget it. I'm calling 911. So help me, if anything happened to Sonny, we're suing. We'll take the owners of this place to the cleaners." She tapped the screen and punched in her passcode. "He could be dead in there and we're wasting time."

The clerk held up the key. "225 you said?"

Much better. Funny how the threat of lawsuits and dead bodies motivated people.

Tim nodded. "Yes. Sonny Peppers."

The guy made quick work of checking his manifest and the name of the guest. "Follow me."

As he hustled around the desk, Lucie met Tim's eye and winked. Her man gritted his teeth. Clearly, he hadn't appreciated her contributions. Lucky for him, she didn't need a lot of stroking when it came to her successes.

The clerk hit the outside steps with Lucie and Tim on his heels. "Thanks for doing this," Tim said, the words rushed enough to indicate a low level of panic. "He's been unstable these last couple days."

No kidding. Unstable might be the perfect descriptor of someone willing to kidnap a woman off the street in daylight.

They reached the second floor balcony and Lucie glanced at the empty Escalade golf cart. By now, Dad would be hiding in the breezeway just beyond room 225 with Ro stationed at the opposite end. Joey? Anyone's guess. But he'd promised to keep an eye on his phone and warn them if Sonny decided to return.

The clerk paused at Sonny's room and stared at the door as if the weight of the situation had finally hit him. Guilt hit Lucie like a kick to the ribs. They'd made this poor guy a pawn in their little investigation, lying to him about a potential dead body.

Just as she opened her mouth, to assure him he didn't have to go in, he turned, key at the ready in his trembling hand. "Since you're not listed on the room registration, I can't let you in. You'll have to wait outside."

Tim gestured to the clerk's hand. "Are you sure you want to do this? I can go in."

"Company policy. I have to."

Hopefully he wouldn't wet himself while adhering to that policy.

Squaring his shoulders, he shoved the key in the lock, flipped it, and pushed the door open before removing it again. Light spilled from the room and the clerk peered inside.

"Hello?"

No answer. As expected. Still, Lucie eased out a breath that wasn't for the clerk's benefit. If there'd been someone in the room, they'd have explaining to do.

Tim held the door open while the clerk checked the bathroom. Lucie peeped inside the wood-paneled room and found it empty except for a duffle bag on top of the green and yellow swirled bedspread. The whole thing was straight out of a seventies sitcom.

Lord, the owners needed to upgrade more than the facade.

Papers were strewn across the long dresser next to the television and she nudged Tim, who'd locked onto the same items. "I know. Looks like a boarding pass."

A second later the clerk reappeared. "He's not here."

"I'll kill him," Lucie said. "He got us all worried and he's not even here."

Tim held a hand up to silence her. Total Golden Globe-nominee action right here. "He said he'd meet us here. Maybe he got hung up somewhere."

Continuing the performance, she tilted her chin up in

defiance. "Well, the least he could do is let us know. I swear, your brother is an inconsiderate moron."

"Wow," the clerk said. "Major league harsh since you made me bust in here to check on him."

"You're right. I'm sorry. He got us all worked up, though. I don't know what to think right now."

The guy waved them from the threshold. "We need to get out."

"Hey!"

Roseanne's voice. Right on cue, coming from the end of the walkway.

Pulling the room key from the lock, the clerk whipped around, ignoring Tim's big hand still holding the door open.

"Are you the guy from the desk?" Ro flapped her arms. Even in the dark it was impossible to miss her bouncing boobs. "This vending machine just stole my five bucks."

The kid groaned. "Not again. I hate that thing. Coming!" He faced Tim. "We need to close the door."

"I'm calling the cops!" Ro shrieked. "I want my snack or my money!"

Lucie slid out of her flip-flop, nudging it inside the door-frame. Who needed Dad and his criminal ways when she had a shoe that could get the job done?

Tim let go of the door. "Thanks for the help."

"Yeah. Sure. Glad we didn't find anything bad."

"Me too."

"Me three," Lucie added from behind the two men.

If this clerk looked at her feet, they were cooked. Cooked!

Whoopsie! Lost my shoe somewhere. In that door? Really? How on earth?

"Sorry to bother you, handsome," Ro said to the clerk, "but I'm *starved.*"

Then she made a little *rowrrrr* noise that put a definite pep in the kid's step. "No problem. Come to the office and I'll reimburse you."

"Swear to God," Tim said, "she's nuts. Totally certifiable."

Before descending the steps, Ro waggled her eyebrows. "Keep him busy," Lucie whispered.

Ro hefted her boobs and saluted. "I'm on it, sister."

As soon as the clerk entered the motel lobby, Tim and Lucie hustled back to Sonny's room, where Joey and Dad had already made themselves useful by searching it.

In full cop mode, Tim stepped inside, slipped his hands into the latex gloves they'd picked up at the pharmacy, and rifled through the bag on the bed. "Anything?"

"No," Dad said. "Drawers are empty. Boarding pass on the dresser. He flew in yesterday. I used a tissue to open the drawers."

"Good. Although, with all the people in and out of here, the place would be a nightmare to get prints from." Tim held up a small spiral bound journal and handed it to Lucie. "Take pictures of the pages while I finish looking in this duffle."

Fully gloved now, Lucie snapped photos of the notes on each page. A kidnapper that kept a diary. Fascinating.

Tim held up the boarding pass for Lucie to snap a picture. "Boston to Palm Beach."

After getting it, Tim set the boarding pass down

"The place is clean," Joey said.

"Luce, you done?"

"Last page." She held it flat and snapped a photo. "Done. Let's scram."

TEN

Dad and Joey filed out of the room followed by Tim and Lucie. If they got out of here without the clerk seeing them, it would be a first for Team Rizzo. Well, Team Rizzo/O'Brien because, holy smokes, Tim had gone along with it. A first for sure.

And, eh-hem, how many people could actually pull off that scam?

Not that it was anything to be proud of, but here she was with her cop boyfriend, mob boss father, and degenerate gambler of a brother talking themselves into some lowlife's hotel room.

Damn, we're good.

"Let's go," Joey said, "before Roseanne pops a few buttons and I gotta beat the crap out of this weasel clerk."

Dad shook his head. "I'll tell ya, she's a pip."

A pip. Seriously? If Lucie had *ever* flashed that much skin, Dad would chain her to the basement post.

"Hey!"

A man strode away from an SUV in the far lane of the

parking lot, his muscular, black-clad form moving like some sort of phantom under the dim lights.

"Dammit," Joey said. "He got back quick."

All Joey had to do was watch his phone and warn them of Sonny's impending return. That was it.

Tim grabbed Lucie's hand, half dragging her down the remaining stairs to the lot. "One job," she hollered at Joey.

"Argue later," Tim said.

If only she'd had her stun gun with her. She'd zap this jerk and be done with it. It was the least he deserved after his attempted kidnapping.

O Sole Mio sounded—*ohmygod with that horn*—and Ro zoomed up with Mom in the passenger seat gripping the roof rail hard enough to snap a few fingers.

"Hop in," Ro said to Dad and Joey. "Let's roll, people!"

Tim grunted. "They're planning a getaway in a golf cart. I'd like to say it's unbelievable, but with this bunch? Anything's possible." He glanced back at Sonny Peppers, still bearing down on them. "Joey, you're with me. Luce, you and your Dad go with Ro. No arguments."

Dad puffed up his chest. "I'm staying with my son. I'll knock this guy's lemon in."

Oh, boy.

She glanced back at Tim whose shoulders seemed to expand ten feet. They must teach that in the police academy. Talk about command presence. This Hulk routine definitely gave the impression he didn't like Dad's plan. "Joe, we need you to stay with the women. Take care of them. Luce! In that cart."

Way to go, O'Hottie. Clearly, she needed to marry this man. Anyone who could order Joe Rizzo around—and survive—was a keeper.

Dad grabbed her hand and she jumped into the rear

seat. She slid over, leaving enough room for him, but before his butt even landed, Ro hit the gas, snapping everyone's head back.

"Ho! Take it easy," Dad said. "You tryin' to kill us?"

"Hey," Sonny Peppers yelled again.

"Hey, what?" Joey held up a hand. "Right here, pal."

Roseanne whipped the cart around, its driver's side wheels lifting from the pavement. Mom crossed herself. "Hail Mary, full of grace..."

They'd need more than prayer for this. "Dad! Lean left."

In time with her father, Lucie threw her weight left. *Eee-doggies*. The ground beside them came closer.

"Hang on," Lucie said.

Bhu-bump, the cart's wheels landed, and Ro did another hairpin turn. Maybe Mom's plan wasn't a bad one.

Hail Mary, full of grace...

"Hey, dopey," Ro hollered at Peppers, drawing his attention from Tim and Joey.

She whooshed by him, flipping him off as she went. Sonny returned the gesture, and Dad started screaming about proper ways to address women. All of it gave Tim and Joey time to move in.

Wheels planted, Ro zoomed into another tight turn around Sonny. Why did this feel like gladiators in the Coliseum?

"Get me in there, Roseanne," Dad said.

"You got it, Mr. R."

What? *Hang on.* "Forget it, Dad, you're on parole. It's a miracle they even let you leave the state. You can't get into a fight."

"She's right, Joe. Stay put."

Ro cut the same direction again. "Joey! I'm coming back around."

Great. *Let's just tell the bad guy our plan.*

Sonny lunged at Tim, who sidestepped and did a quick sweeping move with his leg, knocking Sonny to the ground. Her man. O'Hottie indeed.

"Yeah!" Lucie did a little fast clap.

Sonny hopped to his feet and Ro zoomed by him again, this time way too close. He reached up and grabbed onto the rear roof rail right beside Lucie, his legs bicycling to keep up with the speeding cart. Not one to be taken alive, Ro swerved right, then left. *Right, left, right, left.* Momentum sent them bouncing like some jacked-up gangbanger's car.

Lucie glanced at Mom, whose hair had blown straight back, making her hazel eyes look huge in her head. "Mom, hold on."

"I am," Mom said. "I should have stayed home. Joe, I swear, life with you is never dull. I'm so sick of it."

"This time it's your daughter's fault."

Gee. Thanks, Dad.

"Roseanne," Joey shouted. "Slow down."

Lucie glanced over her shoulder. Tim and Joey gave chase, dodging left and right while Roseanne perfected her golf cart acrobatics.

Pain rocketed through Lucie's skull straight down her neck. "Ow!"

Sonny, in an amazing display of athleticism, held onto the rail with one hand and yanked on Lucie's hair with the other. What the hell was he doing?

Dad slid sideways, chopping at Sonny's hand. "Let go of my baby girl. Do you know who I am?"

Ro did that swerving thing again, which only made things worse. "Ow, ow. *Ow!*"

"Don't worry, Luce," Ro said, "He'll pay. Believe me."

Sonny yanked again.

Enough. She was Joe Rizzo's kid and not about to sit here and let this animal rip her hair out. *Knees.* Tim always told her to go for the throat or knees.

She kicked out—*boom*—blasted him.

He cried out, but still held on. Strong sucker.

"Hit him again, baby girl."

Between Dad's yelling and the adrenaline, Lucie saw red. *Boom.* She kicked him a second time, feeling something in his knee give.

Sonny howled, a long agonizing wail that should've cracked every car window in the lot.

Ro hooked a sharp right, sending him sailing. He hit the pavement with a thump then rolled. Tim and Joey cut left, away from the cart, and stood over Sonny.

The lowlife rocked back and forth, holding his knee. "I think she busted my kneecap."

"So," Tim said, "call a cop. In fact, let's do that. Joey, dial 911. We'll tell them we caught the guy who tried to abduct Lucie. They'll love it."

"On it."

Before Joey even touched his screen, Sonny's eyes bulged. "Wait. Hold on."

"Yeah. That's what I thought." Tim said. "Instead of doing that, we're gonna help your sorry ass up to your room. And then you'll tell us what the hell you're doing here."

Inside Sonny's crappy motel room, Lucie, Mom, and Ro huddled by the door. Tim and Joey sat on the edge of the long dresser. Dad had taken the only chair and sat with one ankle propped over his other knee.

Just a regular night for the Rizzo crew.

Tim crossed his arms and focused on Sonny, sitting on

the bed, his back against the headboard and his legs stretched in front of him with a pillow under his knee.

Sonny met Tim's gaze. "I don't know."

Always the impatient one, Joey threw his hands up. "Do you think we're idiots?"

Dad put both feet on the floor and pointed at Tim. "Give me five minutes with this guy."

"Joe," Mom said, "knock it off. You're always looking to rough someone up."

"Now we know where Joey gets it," Ro quipped.

Lucie snorted, and Tim shot her a look.

"Everyone pipe down." Tim levered off the dresser and walked to the side of the bed, getting right into Sonny's space. "Look, before I unleash these maniacs on you, you'd better start talking."

Sonny looked at Dad and found himself on the receiving end of his famous death stare. Wisely, Sonny went back to Tim. "How the hell did I know she was Joe Rizzo's kid? I was sent here to grab Natalie's."

Now that was truly insulting. "Do I look like I'm in high school?"

He lifted one shoulder. "You kinda do, yeah."

Ro sighed. "I knew you were a dumbass. I really did."

Tim angled back to them, his jaw locked. Her man obviously didn't appreciate the chatter.

"Sorry," Ro and Lucie said in unison.

Tim faced Sonny again. "Dude, this freak show is making me nuts. Do us all a favor and come clean. Someone hired you. You expect me to believe you don't know who?"

"I don't. I swear."

Dad crossed his arms. "Five minutes, Tim. That's all I need."

Any color left in Sonny's face bled out. "Mr. Rizzo, I

swear I ain't lying. The guy who hired me didn't want anyone to know. He sent someone to talk to me."

"An emissary," Lucie said, "interesting."

"A what?"

Joey shook his head. "Jeez, even I know what that is."

Tim once again ignored the chatter and pressed on. "Okay. You used a middleman. They paid you in cash or what?"

"Yeah. We did a drop. They left the money in a garbage can behind a building. Twenty grand to grab Natalie's kid. Once I had her, they'd tell me where to take her." Sonny turned to Dad. "I saw your daughter walking the dog and figured it was her kid. Not yours. Please don't kill me."

Oh, ouch. As much as Lucie liked to avoid thinking about her father's day job, episodes like this reminded her, no matter how civilized and educated she considered herself, she'd always be a mob princess.

Tim snapped his fingers, bringing Sonny's attention back to him. "Hey, focus here. What building did you pick the money up from?"

"Right. Yeah. It's in Boston. I can give you the address." He pointed to his phone sitting on the nightstand where Tim had told him to leave it. "It's in there."

"Fine. And I want the middleman's number, too."

"I don't have it."

Joey made a buzzing noise. "Now he's lying."

"I'm not. I hang out in a bar in Boston. The guy came in. Told me his name was Jerry and he had a job for me. Ten grand up front. The other upon delivery."

"And you don't know who this Jerry is? You just took his word for it? How do you know he wasn't a cop?"

"I didn't. When I took the ten grand, I didn't get arrested so I figured it was legit."

Ro faced Lucie. "Told you he was a dumbass."

By ten o'clock, Lucie knew she wanted a bed. What she couldn't decide on was whether to sleep or jump Tim. The man was an ace. An absolute warrior when it came to getting her out of sticky situations. Quite the aphrodisiac.

After leaving the crappy motel, O'Hottie had artfully managed Sonny's arrest by calling in a tip. In a world full of black SUVs the chances of actually spotting the correct one while driving home from dinner were slim. Beyond slim. Invisible.

The cops didn't need to know that, though. Twelve minutes after Tim's call, the detective in charge of the case notified Lucie they'd caught Sonny turning the rental in at the airport.

The jerk was lamming it. Or attempting to.

Tim unlocked Uncle Henry's front door and pushed it open for her.

"I'm exhausted," she said. "What a day."

"Interesting start to our vacation."

Lucie snorted. "At least it's not my fault. For once."

"There is that."

Inside, swaths of light from the kitchen illuminated the short hallway to the living room.

"He's still up," Tim whispered.

"You bet I am," Henry said. "I'm old, but not deaf."

Poor Henry. The man had to be exhausted. Ignoring the fatigue laying on her like a cement blanket, Lucie headed to the kitchen.

Oh, boy. Henry sat at the table with a half empty bottle of wine in front of him. At least he hadn't gone for the hard stuff.

Yet.

He peered up with a droopy-eyed sadness more than likely attributed to a wicked combination of heartbreak and exhaustion.

"Unc," Tim said, "go to bed. You've had a long day."

"Soon. I'm not drunk yet."

"Switch to bourbon."

Lucie whirled on Tim, holding her hands wide.

"What?" He asked. "It's been a long day. I'm not up for an all-nighter. If he wants to get drunk, he deserves it after this mess of a day. I'm helping him along."

Even as he said it, Tim stared at his phone. While on their stakeout, they'd done a quick internet search for Helen Craft, registered agent. Their efforts resulted in bupkis. Well, not exactly considering the five hundred and forty-three thousand results that'd take days to click through. *Will the real Helen Craft please stand up?* Who knew it was such a common name? All in all, not a big deal. They could contact the secretary of state in Wyoming in the morning.

Or fast track it by using Tim's contacts to find an address for Helen.

He'd been waiting all night for a call back from one of his cop buddies who'd said he'd run Helen's name. Crime being what it was in Chicago, that detective got called out on an armed robbery. Go figure that rotten luck. Could the gangbangers not take a night off?

Lucie gave him a light shove. "Go to bed. I've got this. After that cart ride with Ro, I could use a glass of wine."

Henry cut his eyes between Lucie and Tim. "What ride?"

She grabbed a wineglass from the hanging rack under the cabinet and set it on the table. "Pour and I'll tell you."

Henry smiled, but it was rueful, packed with a whole lot

of...something. Still, he picked up the bottle, gave her a healthy pour, then topped off his own.

"My sister always says you can't trust anyone but family."

Lawdy, that sounded like a Joe Rizzo-ism. "Had she been hanging with my dad?"

That made Henry chuckle. "I don't think so."

Huh. She got a laugh out of him. *Go, Luce!* She held up her glass in toast and took a slug. "And which sister is this? Tim's mom?"

"Yeah. She's a slippery one. Brainwashed all the others. I always thought it was a horrible way to live. Who wants to go through life suspicious of everyone?"

"It's not fun, that's for sure."

Lucie would know. Her entire existence hinged on paranoia. Were the phones tapped? The house bugged? Surveillance outside the house?

For years, she'd avoided going home. The whole idea of the Feds listening in on their family conversations gave her the creeps. Every sound—a pipe knocking, the furnace kicking on, a squirrel on the roof—unleashed a round of paranoia worthy of a Hitchcock flick.

He met her eye, then sat back, dropping his hands to his lap. "Tell me about it."

He knew. At least the public stuff. Being from Chicago, unless he lived in a cave under the city, he'd have heard all the drama. Dad, in his own way, was a local celebrity. The benefactor who donated toys, coats, and food to homeless shelters. And not just at Christmas. All year long—even from prison—he set up toy and food drives in the Rizzo's Italian Beef locations and in their hometown of Franklin. And people gave. Mightily. When Joe spoke, people listened.

Unfortunately, it was for all the wrong reasons.

That was dad.

Good hearted mobster.

And total puzzle.

Lucie fiddled with the stem of her wineglass, dragging her index finger up and down, up and down. "Not much to tell. My father makes his choices. I don't agree with most of them, but he kept us warm in the winter with food in our bellies. We lacked nothing. We weren't abused. Aside from being labeled a mob princess, I had a solid upbringing."

"Tim says you have a master's from Notre Dame."

"I do. In my naive, idealist mind, I thought if I could prove myself, be educated by one of the finest schools in the country, people would see I was different. That Joe Rizzo's daughter was more than what everyone thought."

"How'd that work out?"

"Could be worse. I have a growing, multi-faceted, and extremely *legitimate* business, yet there are days I'm still Lucie Rizzo, mob princess. My mother and I, and to an extent, Joey, are casualties in my father's war with the government." She leaned in, propped her chin in her hand. "I've been judged my whole life by people who don't know me. I try to block out the noise. I can't let it define me."

"It can't be easy."

Lucie smiled. "I have a good man who loves me. If a Chicago cop can hold my hand and walk with his head high, what more do I need?"

A door closing on the other side of the wall drew Henry's gaze. "He was always a smart kid."

And he's all mine. "You know," Lucie said, snapping Henry's attention back. "In a lot of ways, Mattie and I are similar. We're both stuck with the legacy our fathers dumped on us. Doesn't seem fair."

At the mention of Mattie, Henry bolted upright and reached for his wineglass. "You think she's innocent?"

Too soon to tell. But the woman deserved an opportunity to prove herself. "I don't know. All I'm saying is I could see it. When I was young, my father was my world. I adored him. Actually, part of me still does and I'm grateful for that. I can look at him and see the daddy who took me to the beach or for ice cream or threw me in the pool when we went to the Dells. Back then, I believed *everything* he told me. I had no reason not to. As I got older, I'd hear the rumors. I'd see how people treated him. The respect. The fear. It confused me until someone called me a mob princess on the playground. I cried for a week."

"Ack. Kids are vicious. I'm sorry."

Uncle Henry reached across the table, set his hand over hers, and something inside burst open. Just a flood of love for a man she barely knew but would, hopefully, one day be family.

"It is what it is. I grew a thick skin. Another thing I'm thankful for."

He let go and, before relaxing back in his chair, took a long pull of his wine. Who said it was meant to be sipped?

"You think I should give Mattie another chance?"

"I think you should talk to her. Really talk to her. If she's been duped by her father and put in danger as a result, she's a victim. If she's a willing participant and running from the law, that's a different story. We're trying to help find the truth, but aside from caring about you, we don't have a dog in this fight. You're the one in love. You need to figure out if you can stand by her, ride out the storm. And, believe me, that's pressure. It'll test you in ways you won't even see coming. Depending on how big this is, friends will disappear. Reporters might chase you or call begging for a sound bite. Who knows?"

Henry let out the long sigh of a man unsure of his

resolve. If he loved Mattie, really loved her, could he deal with the chaos?

Lucie paused, held up her hands, "I'm probably way out of line here, but I love your nephew. His family is important to him and that makes you important to me."

"Say it."

Heaven help her if this was the wrong thing to say, but... "Mattie's alone in this. How will you feel if she turns out to be innocent and you turned your back on her?"

A long pause drifted between them, the silence lingering. And lingering. And lingering.

At least until Henry's phone bleeped. He checked the screen, then picked it up, his lips dipping into a tight frown.

"What is it?"

"It's Mattie. She sent a link." He poked at the screen. "It's a news report." He peered up at Lucie and held the phone out. "From Boston."

Lucie snatched the phone away. Onscreen was a paused video. She tapped the little arrow and waited. Buffering, buffering, buffering. *Come on.*

Finally, the video rolled revealing a blond haired man in a suit standing at a podium. The caption at the bottom read "BREAKING NEWS: Boston District Attorney, Simon Torrance press conference. Arrest made in conspiracy case linking Boston developers to That Girl fraud."

No, no, no. Lucie dropped her head to the table. "It's a press conference."

"Cliff," the man onscreen said, "I can't comment on that. Next question."

"What about other conspirators?" Someone shouted. "Is Paul Landon still a suspect?"

Torrance nodded. "Mr. Landon, along with several others I won't name, continue to be persons of interest.

We're looking at everyone. This is a major retailer who employs a lot of people around the country. Fraud of this level could cripple a company and we're not letting it go. We're going after everyone who was even remotely involved." Torrance flipped his portfolio closed and picked it up. "That's all for now. We'll update you as necessary. Any further questions can be forwarded to our media relations department. Thank you all. Goodnight."

*Good*night? Ha! *Horrible* is more like it.

Henry shot out of his chair, knocking it backward and sending it crashing to the floor with a *thwack*. "Dammit."

When he wobbled, Lucie leaped up and gripped his arm. "Whoa, Henry. Take it easy. Do you want help getting to your room?"

"No. I need to see her. Mattie. Right now. I need my keys."

Um, no. If the man couldn't get up from a chair without falling over, he shouldn't be driving. At all.

"You've been drinking. You can't."

"Then you'll drive me."

I will?

He grabbed her hand and squeezed. "Please, Lucie. Take me there. Before it's too late."

ELEVEN

Lucie hit the brakes in Mattie's driveway a split second before Henry jumped out and high-tailed it to her front door. For an older guy, he could move.

Interior lights glowed through a slit in the drapes. With the number of spotlights in front of her house, a 747 pilot might mistake it for a runway.

Lit up as it was, no one would get close without being seen. Which, Lucie supposed, was the point.

Life on the run.

Lucie shifted to park. "I'll wait here. Take your time."

On his way to the door, Henry turned back. "Come inside. You can't be out here alone. Not after what happened."

Point there. But, hello? This might be a *tad* awkward.

Awkward or not, she intended on not getting kidnapped and followed Henry to Mattie's door, checking her surroundings as she went, scanning the bushes for any Sonny wannabes.

Rather than ring the bell, Henry rapped on the door. "It's me. Open up."

A second later, the door slid open and Henry paddled his hand at Lucie. "Hurry up. Step on it."

Yeesh.

Once inside, Mattie closed and bolted the door. Next to it sat two large suitcases and a carry-on. Lucie didn't need her master's degree to know what that meant.

Henry gave them a long, pensive look, then lifted his chin to Mattie. "What are you doing?"

For a brief few seconds, she met Lucie's gaze then let it bounce to the ceiling, the floor, the suitcases. Anywhere but Henry.

"Leaving," she said, eyes still on the cases. "I have to go. They've found me. And now this arrest has brought everything back to the public eye. I'm not safe. And neither are you. I put Lucie in danger. I can't live with that."

"And what? You were going to leave? Not a word? And for God's sake look at me. I deserve that much at least."

She snapped her head up. "You deserved a lot more, Henry. More than me, by far. I'd have called from the road. I won't have you or your family in danger because of me."

"What about you? You can't battle this on your own."

Unsure how much to contribute, Lucie nodded. *Way to step to the plate, mister.* And then, well, what the hell? "He's right. If you stay, you have a support system."

Mattie eyed her. "Of all people, I can't believe you're saying that. You were almost abducted."

"But I wasn't."

"Right," Henry said. "And we have an update on the kidnapper. Tell her, Lucie."

Me? "Uh, okay."

Again, Mattie cut her gaze to the suitcases then faced Lucie. "I don't have time for this. Please, I have to go."

"Where?"

"Atlanta."

Henry cocked his head. "*Atlanta?* Why?"

"I can't fly anywhere. Paul Landon knows my new name. I'll have to disappear. I'll drive to Atlanta, make sure I wasn't followed and get on a train to California. I already took Aphrodite to the kennel. When I settle in somewhere, I'll send for her." She held Henry's gaze. "I have to pick up my daughter and we'll run again. To Mexico. Or Canada. I don't know," she cried.

Lucie shook her head. All this running. Having lived under the Rizzo spotlight, there'd been plenty of occasions Lucie considered getting in her car and taking off without a word. At one time, she'd begged her ex, Frankie, another mob kid, to move to New York with her. Start over in a city not so caught up in her father's day-to-day drama.

But Frankie, as much as he'd loved her, he couldn't leave. At least not then. If only she'd been ESPN. When *they* offered him a job, he sure took off in a hurry.

Bitterness filled her mouth and she swallowed hard. *Forget that.*

She shook it off. It was for the better.

"Mattie," she said, "how long can you do this?"

"What?"

"Live like this. Moving every few months and constantly covering your tracks in case Paul Landon, or whoever is after you, catches up. It's not fair to you or your daughter."

"I have no choice."

"It's not a life," Henry added.

Lucie stepped forward, angling around Henry to grasp Mattie's hands. "I can't possibly understand. None of us could. But I know what it feels like to want to hide. To disappear for a while. You shouldn't have to live this way because your father screwed up. Believe me, I tell myself that often."

"Does it work?"

Lucie smiled. "Sometimes. I made a choice a couple years ago. I could go with the poor-me scenario or move past it."

"How?"

"By figuring out that my father's bad decisions are not my fault. I won't take that on. It's stifling and frustrating and...well...exhausting. My dad won't change and once I accepted that, I figured out how to be Lucie Rizzo, entrepreneur instead of mob princess."

"This is different."

"It sure is. But you have a choice. Right now the universe has thrown a crossroad in front of you. You can run from a place you seem to love." Lucie glanced back at Henry. "And the man who comes with it. Or you can stay and fight. We'll help you. Tim is a great detective. He understands the law. And, hello, have I mentioned my father has one of the country's greatest criminal defense attorneys?"

Believe me, sister. I've needed him a lot recently.

Henry cleared his throat. "Innocent people shouldn't run. *You* shouldn't."

For a few seconds, Mattie stood still, her eyes locked on Henry. Holy cow the pressure. If she turned away, game over. She'd break Henry's heart and then Lucie would have to kill her. Bury her body in a swamp somewhere.

One with a lot of gators.

Finally, she let out a hard breath that sent her ample boobs bouncing. "I don't know how to fight this," she said, her voice sailing up an octave. "It's...a lot."

Henry moved closer. "Honey, listen to what Lucie found out. Then decide."

Mattie blinked, eyes shimmering with moisture, and it kicked Lucie straight in the chest.

Ach.

Maybe the gators were overkill.

How many times had Lucie gotten into hijinks that should've sent Tim racing to the door? No matter what, he'd stood by her. Loyalty, apparently, ran in the family because Henry, probably confused, angry, and hurt all at once, still found it inside him to call this woman honey.

A good man. Just like his nephew.

Lucie held up a hand. "He's right. Hear me out. You at least owe me that much." She smiled. "What with almost getting me kidnapped and all."

Guilt. As much as she hated to employ it, got the job done.

Mattie snorted. "You're something else, Lucie. I'll give you ten minutes. Then I have to go."

Ha.

They'd see about that.

The deadline came and went. Yet here they were, still parked on Mattie's sofa while she took in all that Lucie had just shared. The stakeout, the search of Sonny's room, the boarding pass from his Boston to Palm Beach flight. Lucie kicking the crap out of Sonny and his subsequent admissions, all of it laid out carefully for Mattie to dissect.

When Lucie emptied her brain of all things related to Sonny Peppers, Mattie threw her hands up, smacking them against her skintight jeans. "He expects us to believe he doesn't know who hired him?"

"As nutty as it sounds, my dad said it's possible." *Dad would know. Sigh.*

"What's the address of the building he spoke of?"

Lucie checked her phone and read it off.

"Huh."

Placing one hand on Henry's knee, more a gesture of familiarity than anything, Mattie levered up from her spot and quick-walked to her suitcases. She'd better not be skipping out. Not without some sort of response other than *huh*.

But, surprise, surprise, rather than head out the door, she pulled a laptop from her carry-on, bringing it back to the sofa and booting it up.

"At work," she said, "we'd use Boston's property assessment website to check the values of listings. The owners are there and if their address is different from the property, it'll list both."

Oh, brilliant. Lucie pushed out of her chair and moved behind the sofa to look over Mattie's shoulder.

Mattie's fingers flew over the keyboard—she must have aced typing class. A screen popped up welcoming them to the site. Mattie typed the address into the search box and...*Voila*. A new page popped up with type small enough to convince Lucie a trip to the eye doctor might be in her future. She leaned in and squinted as she scanned.

Property type: commercial. Value: $875,000.

Come on, where are you?

She continued reading and...bingo.

Owner: Paul Landon.

Mattie straightened her shoulders, closed the laptop, and stood. "I have to go."

Whoa. Hang on. Before Mattie took a step, Lucie ran to the suitcases and held her hands up. Childish? Sure. Did she care?

No.

Dog-tired and short on patience, she couldn't worry about her maturity level.

"Just hold on," Lucie said. "It shouldn't be a shock that Landon owns that building."

"Oh, it's not. It confirms that I need to go. Move."

Nice try, lady. Not happening. "Let's call Tim. He'll know what to do. Please. Don't leave before we muddle through this."

Without waiting for an answer, Lucie whipped out her phone. "Give me two minutes."

Phone to her ear, Lucie shifted right, standing directly in Mattie's path.

"No," Mattie said. "Move."

Lucie held up a finger. "It's ringing. One sec."

Before the second ring, Tim picked up. "Ugh," he said, his voice groggy from disturbed sleep. "Why are you calling me from the kitchen?"

"I'm not in the kitchen."

"I was afraid you'd say that."

"Hey. Don't give me a hard time. Henry wanted to see Mattie and he'd been drinking. I couldn't let your uncle drive while under the influence, could I?"

"Or maybe you both could've waited until morning?"

No one would ever accuse Tim of being a romantic, that was for sure. "Listen, Romeo, if you'd let me, I can give you information before Mattie lams it again. And I'm not being dramatic. As we speak, her bags are lined up at the door and she's ready to blow right through me to get out of here."

The classic Tim sigh streamed through the phone line. "What have you got, Columbo?"

That was more like it. When Mattie shifted right to circumvent her, Lucie sidestepped. No one was leaving until

Tim weighed in. "The building Sonny Peppers said he picked up the money from is owned by Paul Landon."

"Hunh," Tim said.

"Is that a good hunh or a bad hunh?" At times, like now, it was hard to tell.

"It's a non-committal hunh."

Terrific. Lucie smacked herself on the forehead. Could she get a break here? "What does that even mean?"

On the other end a rustling noise, the unmistakable sound of covers being tossed aside, filled the silence. "It means I'll be there in ten minutes. Don't do anything until I get there. And tell Mattie to stay put. I'm tired and cranky. Chasing her down in the middle of the night would piss me off."

Lucie squeezed her eyes shut, fought the fatigue fogging her brain. "It has to be him who sent Sonny, right?"

"Luce, if this guy is any kind of a decent criminal, which he must be if the Feds have yet to charge him, he won't pay a hitman by leaving the money at his own damned building."

Darn it. She smacked herself again. How had she missed that? "You think it's—"

"—a setup? Yeah. Someone is framing Paul Landon."

"I HAD A THOUGHT," Lucie said from her spot on the sofa when Tim strode through Mattie's door.

He circled around, kissed the top of her head, and dropped next to her. "Can't wait."

Oh, ha-ha.

She should wallop him for being a smart mouth, but he looked so adorably rumpled in a wrinkled T-shirt and basketball shorts that she couldn't do it. The kicker was his hair. He wore it close-cropped, but long enough that after sleeping the velvety red strands mashed down on the right side. That's what being a side-sleeper got him. He'd attempted to throw some water on his head and fix it, but what she loved about her man was that he didn't care what he looked like when a crisis loomed. Tim was all about action and getting things done.

Even if his hair wouldn't cooperate.

In the eight minutes it took him, she'd had a brainstorm and quickly commandeered the laptop. Yes, it was after midnight, but her strung out mind and body had reached that pivotal point when fatigue morphs into twisted mania that'd keep her going for hours.

She tapped the screen. ""You'll love this, big boy. Wyoming Secretary of State's website."

"Okay. I'd planned on calling them in the morning."

"Well, Detective, why wait when we can—wait for it—download a *list* of *all* companies registered in the fine state of Wyoming." She threw her arms up in triumph.

Tim's eyebrows hitched. A spark of his tenacious need for the truth lit his green eyes. "Seriously?"

"Yep. Mattie showed me a website with Boston property tax assessments. It got me thinking, so I did a search for owners of Wyoming companies. That brought me to this website. It should give us contact information for owners and registered agents."

He high-fived her and something churned low and deep in her belly. Ninety-eight point five percent of the time, Tim poo-pooed her investigations. Not that he doubted her intellect or skill. He simply hated her putting herself in tenuous situations that might get her hurt. Or worse.

A high-five from Tim? She might as well have won the Nobel Peace Prize.

A few taps later, Lucie watched the download bar crawl.

"Big file," Tim said.

"Sure is. With any luck, we can sort it by registered agents."

Tick, tock, tick, tock. Almost downloaded.

Tim craned his neck to look down the short hallway leading to the back of the house. "Where's Uncle Henry and Mattie?"

"They went to her room to talk. This has devastated him, Tim."

"My mom will freak."

Again with his mother? Lucie liked the woman—a lot—but certain boundaries shouldn't be crossed. "Yeah, well, all due respect, it's not her life. What if Mattie is innocent? Henry would be turning his back on the woman he loves."

He did the Tim sigh. Well, too bad. Someone had to think of Henry's emotional vulnerability in all this.

"Luce, I hear you. But I don't know what to think."

"The frustrated mob princess side of me thinks Mattie got the shaft. I could be wrong, but I have a feeling about this one."

"And if you are?"

She couldn't go there. Being wrong scared the you-know-what out of her. "I don't know. But we need to give her a chance."

Lucie glanced at the screen. *Download complete.* She clicked the file, watched the wheel spin for an agonizing fifteen seconds until a spreadsheet—a mess of one—popped up.

Tim leaned forward. "The columns are all screwed up. You can't sort it like that."

An understatement for sure. Not only were the headers not matching up with the corresponding columns, some of the fields had merged. "Don't panic."

"Uh, I'm a Chicago cop, if spreadsheets scared me, I'd be committed by now."

Always appreciative of Tim's gallows humor, Lucie snorted. *So cute, her man.* "We can search the spreadsheet for Helen Craft. If she's in here, we copy the data to a clean sheet and in the morning start calling the numbers."

"Good," he said. "Let's do it."

"This is fun, isn't it?"

"My uncle's life going down the crapper?"

"Not that. Working together. I like it."

He flashed the O'Brien smile and locked those lush greens on her. "Me too. I love you, Luce."

If she wasn't so tired, he'd totally get lucky after this.

"I love *you*, Detective."

She leaned over and planted one on him. Right in Mattie's living room, just bam. This wasn't a ho-hum, casual kiss either.

Open mouths and tongues were involved.

She angled her head, giving him and his fabulous tongue better access. *Totally getting lucky, later.*

His hand came around, settling on her hip. He gave her a squeeze and slowly pulled back. "We're in the middle of something here and you do this to me? You're evil."

"I know." *Bad, Lucie. Bad.*

Such a slut. But she'd rocked his world—and maybe specific parts of his anatomy Lucie had grown fond of.

Lucie shook off the buzz left by Tim's lips and focused on the spreadsheet, cracking her knuckles as she read. "Quit distracting me. We have things to do. Search term: Helen Craft."

She typed the name in and the cursor went to the first entry for Helen Craft.

"Boom," Tim said. "Got one."

"Yep."

Lucie copied the row into a new spreadsheet and clicked back to the original list. She clicked the search arrow again.

Helen Craft.

"That's two," Tim said.

The second was copied into the new spreadsheet and Lucie repeated the exercise. Thirteen times.

When all entries had been exhausted, Lucie slouched against the back of the sofa, the laptop still resting on her legs.

Tim peered back at her. "Different addresses all over the state." He waggled a finger. "It doesn't say her company's name."

"No. Just Helen Craft."

Tim sat back, rested his head on the cushion while he stared up at the ceiling. Thinking. "We can't assume she doesn't own a management company."

"Remember that scandal last year. The law firm?"

He looked at her. "The one that helped their clients hide billions in overseas accounts?"

"Yes. Their sole function was to be a registered agent for wealthy people trying to evade taxes. That's all they did. The entire firm."

"If Helen Craft was on that level, she'd have more than thirteen companies."

True. Damn him. Lucie grunted.

Still mulling it over, Tim went back to studying the ceiling. "Let's break it down. She's working for someone, say Paul Landon, whose son happens to be the in-house real estate guy for a major US retailer. For shits and giggles, we'll say it's That Girl. Daddy—being Paul Landon—connects the developers with his son. Or daddy partners with them. They buy buildings in certain markets."

Ooh, ooh. Lucie raised her hand. "Certain markets where That Girl has stores."

Tim smiled and tweaked her nose. "So smart, you are. Daddy is the secret middleman, though. His name can't be anywhere near this thing due to the whole nepotism conflict. The developers buy buildings and lease space to That Girl for way over market price."

"Which drives up the selling price for the building. Those lease deals are a pot of gold."

"It's not about the That Girl lease. These guys are looking ahead. They put the building on the market and up the selling price. They justify it by telling potential buyers they'll make a fortune on the That Girl lease. Dang, that's slick."

Developers. Middlemen. Market manipulation. All of it swooped through Lucie's mind, the investment banker in her connecting dots. *Oh, wow.* She sat up so fast, momentum sent the laptop tipping. *Whoopsie.* She snatched it before it tumbled to the floor and set it on the table.

Tim set his hand on her back. "What are you thinking?"

Did he have a week? That might not even be enough time for the thoughts raging in her mind. She peered over her shoulder at him. "We need to link Helen Craft with any companies Mattie and her dad did business with. Then see if we can link them back to someone besides Paul Landon."

TWELVE

On a quest to find the printer she'd just sent her spreadsheet to, Lucie summoned Mattie, who led her to the second bedroom that doubled as an office. Like the rest of the house, everything was neat, tidy, and well-styled, but...somehow bare. Too perfect. Nothing about the interior said home. Lived-in. Maybe Lucie and Tim could help Mattie change that.

On the desk in the corner, the printer whirred and spit out two pages.

Mattie scooped them up and read them. "What's this?"

"The thirteen companies in Wyoming Helen Craft is a registered agent for. Island Management is on there." Lucie waved her to the living room where Tim and Uncle Henry waited. "I'd like to go through this list with you and see if we can link any of the other companies to you or your father."

"Why?"

"It's a long shot, but if we can make a link, maybe we can identify who else was involved in the fraud."

They entered the living room, where Henry sat on the

overstuffed loveseat adjacent to the sofa. "Do you think that's who might be after Mattie?"

Tim took the list from Mattie and read it over again. "Or at least involved with Paul Landon. Right now, all we have is Sonny Peppers picking up his payment from Landon's building. It feels too convenient to me."

Mattie made a move toward Henry, but paused, obviously rethinking her seating options while she and Tim pretended the level of awkwardness hadn't just risen to epic heights. Finally, after Lucie contemplated stabbing herself, Mattie turned and sat in the lone side chair anchoring the loveseat and sofa.

"Dad handled most of the That Girl business. But—" she held up a finger, "—I have a report showing all commissions paid to us last year. I handled all reporting for our taxes. It's in a folder on my computer."

"Can we look at it?"

"Of course."

Mattie grabbed the laptop from the coffee table and zipped away on the keyboard. Seconds later, she handed it to Lucie, who sat with Tim on the sofa. Together, they skimmed the spreadsheet.

Lucie circled a finger at the screen where rows and rows of commissions had been listed. "Do you mind if I play with this? I'll create a copy, so I don't mess anything up."

"Go ahead. And thank you." She glanced at Tim then back to Lucie. "Both of you. Not a lot of people would trust me. You're amazing people."

Lucie shrugged. "On a certain level, you and I understand each other. And Tim? He loves his uncle. That's what people who care do. They support one another." She smiled at Tim. "It's one of the many reasons I love him."

Tim ripped off a smile that let her know the feeling was

more than mutual. His green eyes lit with the hunger that came right before the two of them typically shared an orgasm or twelve. Fatigue or not, O'Hottie would get lucky after this. It might be a quickie, but he'd have a smile on that handsome face when she finished with him.

Heat rushed into Lucie's cheeks. *Oooh-eeee.* The man riled her up. Tim let out a soft snort. *Focus here, Luce.* She peeled her gaze away, forcing it back to the laptop, where she copied the file and saved it. A quick sort alphabetized the corporation names. Here we go. "Tim, read me the thirteen company names from the Wyoming list."

"Sure. First one. Garnett Inc."

Lucie jumped to the Gs on the laptop screen. Nothing. Shoot. "Nope. Next one."

"Jefferson Davis, LLC."

Nothing. *Dang it.* "Nope. Next one."

They repeated the exercise two more times, each being a bust. They could be way off base here. Maybe Mattie's father and Geoffrey Landon did indeed work on their own to defraud That Girl. But then who was after Mattie?

"Luce," Tim said, "We've got nine more to check. Next name: Dilford Management."

She stabbed at the arrow key, zipped up too far to the Cs. *Shoot.* She needed to settle in here, slow her brain down and focus on right now. This very second. No looking ahead. In the moment. That's what she'd be. In. The. Moment.

Nine more names. Nine more opportunities. *Got this.* She touched the arrow key again and tap-tap-tapped her way to the companies starting with D.

DDC, Dawson, Denlin, Dickerson, Dilford.

Whoa. *Yes!* She pumped a fist. "Kids, we have a Dilford."

Tim read off the address and Lucie nodded as she scrolled right on the spreadsheet. "Mattie, this doesn't tell us who the owners of the company are or who authorized the payments. Do you have that somewhere?"

Mattie paddled her hands and Lucie passed the laptop over. "We scan all the contracts."

She did her thing then handed it back to Lucie who scrolled to the document's signature page. "Authorized signature is Anderson Bort. Do you know him?"

"No."

Lucie jotted the name and corporation. "He doesn't necessarily have to be the owner. He could be someone authorized by them. We'll research him later." She closed the file and clicked back to her spreadsheet. "Tim, give me the next name on your list."

It took two more names before they got another hit. "Fontina Capital, LLC," Lucie said. "Got it."

Rather than pass the laptop back and forth, Mattie jumped up from her chair and joined Lucie and Tim on the sofa. Lucie angled enough for Mattie to find the pdf of the scanned contract. She read off the name of the authorized representative and Lucie jotted it down, the two of them working together with Tim to get through the list.

Clearly inspired by their makeshift investigative team, Henry rose from the loveseat and sat on the sofa arm next to Tim. "I don't know what I can do, but I'm here if you need me."

Lucie smiled at him. "Teamwork, people. It's a beautiful thing."

By the end, they had four corporations from the Wyoming list that paid commissions to Mattie and her father's agency. Some of Lucie's angst over the earlier dead ends broke away. Four companies might not be a gold mine of intel, but they had a start.

From his spot beside Lucie, Tim leaned forward so he

could see Mattie. "Can we confirm if these deals involved That Girl?"

Mattie perked up, cocking her head. "I can look at the property addresses and see if there are That Girl stores in those buildings."

"Store locator." Lucie opened a browser and went to the That Girl website. "Give me the zip codes."

In the three minutes it took to match all the building locations with That Girl stores, the pieces started coming together. Only Lucie couldn't quite figure out what they meant.

"So, what we have," she said, "is the same registered agent managing what could be shell companies that have bought buildings with valuable leasing deals involving That Girl stores."

Tim shook his head. "I need to put this on paper. Mattie, got a notebook?"

Nearly leaping from the sofa, she hustled to the kitchen, her rear swinging in her tight jeans. In Lucie's mind, burlesque music sounded, and she hummed along, receiving an odd look from Tim. *Whoopsie.* She rolled her lips in. *Bad Lucie.* But, holy moly, she might be looking at a version of Ro in twenty-five years.

For some reason, it made her smile.

Mattie walked back, minus the burlesque music—thank you very much—and set a pen and legal pad on the coffee table.

Tim leaned forward and wrote That Girl at the top, circling it. "Here's the retailer." He drew a line off to the side. "Here's Geoffrey Landon, in-house real estate exec." He drew another below Geoffrey's name. "Mattie's father."

Lucie waggled her finger at the drawing. "Paul Landon. We need one for him."

Paul Landon was added with two lines connecting him to Geoffrey and Mattie's father.

"The developers," Henry said. "Who do we connect them to?"

We. Excellent. *Go, Henry.*

"Good question," Tim said.

Lucie studied the names on the diagram. *What's missing?* Something. Some connection that linked it all together. She glanced at the list of thirteen companies Tim had set on the table and...yep. She snapped her fingers. "Helen Craft. She's the registered agent for the shell company Mattie's dad created, plus the other four companies that have leasing deals with That Girl. They're all connected to Mattie's real estate firm."

Tim added Helen Craft's name with spokes to Mattie's father and the four developers. "You said Paul Landon arranged for your dad to meet developers. Could he have arranged these deals? I still think it's too convenient to be him, but the fact that Sonny's money drop happened at one of Landon's buildings makes me think someone connected to him is involved."

"It seems logical," Lucie said.

"We need proof. Mattie, is there anything—anything at all—connecting Paul Landon to your father?"

Mattie let out a long breath. "I don't know. I'm such a fool. All this was going on right in front of me and I didn't know. I swear I didn't *know*."

Lucie slipped an arm around her. "*Ssshhh.* It's okay. We just need to connect the dots.

Tim sat back, scrubbed two hands over his face. Mental and physical fatigue was obviously setting in.

Beside Tim, Henry's shoulders drooped. Her A-Team needed rest. Lucie closed the laptop. "I think we've made great progress here. Why don't we take a break? All of us get some sleep and we'll reconvene in the morning. Our minds will be fresh, and we'll be able to think."

Tim picked up his pen again and tapped it against Paul Landon's name. "We need to connect him to—" he tapped the area where he'd written the four developers businesses, "—them. That's the goal."

"Good *mornnnnn*-ing!"

Lucie, snuggled quite nicely with Tim curled against her back, squeezed her eyes closed. Had to be a dream. Had to be. How else would Roseanne be screaming inside Henry's house?

"Buongiorno! Bonjour. Guten morgen. Wakey-wakeyyyyy."

In Henry's house screaming in foreign languages.

"Kill me," Tim muttered, his voice hoarse from sleep.

"I'm sorry. I was hoping it was a dream."

"Nightmare is more like it. What the hell time is it?"

Lucie forced her crusty eyes open and blinked against the sunlight peeping through the curtains. Lawdy, that hurt. She peered at the green glare of the digital clock, blinking until it came into focus. "Eight twenty-three."

"Why is she here so early?"

"You know her. She wants to get as much in as she can. And, in her defense, she doesn't know we were up half the night."

"Helllooooo! Where is everybody?"

"Can you get rid of her? I gotta sleep another hour. At least."

Lucie tossed back the covers and patted his arm. "I'm on it. Go back to sleep."

Her suitcase sat on the floor near the windows. She grabbed the first bra, shorts, and T-shirt she found in case Henry was out there somewhere. She didn't need Tim's uncle staring at her in her ripped Notre Dame sleep T-shirt.

After jamming her feet into her favorite fuzzy slippers, Lucie whipped the bedroom door open. She strode down the hall, passing Henry's bedroom. Bed made. Where the heck was he with Ro yelling like that?

"Luuucccieeee?"

For the love of God. She swung around the wall and came face to face with Ro in the living room, looking stunning in a pair of white silky shorts, a teal tank top, and a lightweight sweater. All paired with six-inch man-killer heels. Throw in her coiffed hair and perfect makeup and Lucie looked like a schlump by comparison. One who just rolled out of bed. "*Ssshhh.* Tim is still sleeping. We were up late."

"Is that code for you were banging each other all night? You know I love the details."

Leave it to Ro. "Uh, no. It's code for Mattie is in a mess and we were trying to figure out how to get her out of it. Where's Henry?"

"No idea. I knocked, but no one answered. The door was unlocked so I came in."

A flash of blue beyond the rear door caught Lucie's eye. She moved closer and spotted Henry, wearing a navy shirt, pacing the yard, cell phone to his ear.

"He's on the phone out back."

"What's up with Mattie? And, dear God, Luce, really, you should brush your hair before meeting guests."

"You're not a guest. You're Ro."

Her BFF gave her a sugary smile. "Awww. Sweet. You're still a disaster."

"Why are you here so early?"

"We're in Florida. We should walk on the beach. Get a little girl time. Plus, your brother is driving me crazy. Do you know he's horny all the time? I swear, I can't get a break with him."

Who was she kidding? She loved it. "Um, no. Can't say I knew that about my *brother*. I mean, ew!" Lucie gagged. "And, really? Walking on the beach in that outfit? The heels might be a problem."

"Oh, hardy-har. I'll take them off, smartass. I swear, you Rizzos. Everything is a debate."

Obviously she and Joey had yet another fight, because suddenly all Rizzos were included in whatever nonsense the two of them had going on. And one thing Lucie didn't like was being lumped in. At least not when she wasn't even sure what she was being lumped in with.

"What happened this time? Another remark about the size of your ass? Making lewd comments in public? Some stupid theory on why women should stay in the kitchen?"

Joey may not have been the face that launched a thousand ships, but he was definitely the mouth that launched a thousand wars.

Ro circled a hand in the air. "I don't know. He's so...so... alpha. All the time."

"I thought you liked that about him."

"I do. But it's irritating."

Lucie laughed. "You two are nuts."

"What else is new?"

Outside, Henry still wandered the yard, phone to his ear, his free hand occasionally lifting and then flopping again. Despite his slow movements, his shoulders appeared stiff. Forced. A man carrying the world's weight. And who would he be talking to this early?

Ro stepped up beside Lucie, the two of them watching Henry. "What's going on with him? Don't tell me there's another Sonny Peppers."

"No. At least not that I know of, but you make a good point. With Sonny out, whoever sent him might dispatch yet another empty-headed loser. This thing has totally hijacked my vacation. All I wanted was pina coladas and Tim for ten days and here we were up the whole night for all the wrong reasons."

"What happened?"

Ha. Where to start? Lucie gave Ro the three-minute summation of last night's activity, even showing her the chart Tim drew connecting all the participants.

"Luce," Ro said, "how do you get into this stuff?"

"Tell me about it. All I know is it's no coincidence Helen Craft is the registered agent for a group of companies that leased or bought commercial real estate with That Girl stores inside."

"So, what now?"

"We have to find the link between all the companies. It all seems to hang on Paul Landon, but Tim thinks he's too convenient. That it's a frame-up."

"His son is the real estate buyer for That Girl. This guy would have to be an idiot, which—" Ro waved a hand, "—is not out of the question with men. Still, he'd have to be a top-tier idiot to do funky real estate deals involving his son's company."

"Idiot or not, his name isn't on any of the incorporation papers. I think they formed a shell company, so they could hide his identity. Shells make it easy to do that."

"Ha! *You're* telling *me*? I learned the hard way with that damned stripper-banger of an ex-husband."

Lucie blew air threw her lips. The rat-bastard stripper-banger.

When Lucie failed to respond, her majesty the Drama Queen flapped her arms. "Luce! Tell me you forgot. You're my bestie and *that* was a major part of my divorce!"

Stripper-banger. Shell company. Divorce.

Got it.

"Of course I didn't forget. It just took me a second."

"Good." Ro brought her fists up, squeezing so hard she might pop something. "All men are scum."

A long sigh sounded, and Lucie angled back to find Tim shuffling toward the kitchen, more than likely in search of coffee.

He held up a hand in greeting. "The stripper-banger, I presume?"

"Good guess," Lucie said.

"Scum," Ro cried.

Divorce. Shell Company. *Hold on.* Lucie paused, letting her mind circle whatever idea might be forming. *Come on, come on. What is it?*

Divorce.

Shell Company.

Hiding assets.

In the kitchen, Tim grabbed a mug from a cabinet and must have found the coffee pot full. "Nectar of the gods. Thank you."

"Wait," Lucie said. "She's got something here."

He held the mug up. "Aside from men being scum?"

Smart-mouthing so early. Excellent. Rather than encourage that behavior, she'd ignore it. "During their divorce, the stripper-banger tried to hide assets."

Tim grinned. Lucie knew that look all too well. As much as he liked to pretend Ro annoyed him, he secretly enjoyed winding her up and watching the explosion. "I guess he didn't want to fund Ro's Gucci obsession."

Ro gasped. "Scum! Ooh, just thinking about it burns me up. That cheap bastard. He formed a company, put his friend's name on all the paperwork to shield his identity, and made fake invoices to show the IRS the *company* was losing money. Meanwhile, our assets were parked there, waiting for my divorce settlement to be final."

Mug in hand, Tim walked back to the living room and settled into Uncle Henry's favorite chair. "Wow. He *is* scum."

"Thank you, O'Hottie."

"You're welcome. I'm guessing by your wardrobe you busted him before the divorce was final."

"You know it. My lawyer was good. He hired a forensic accountant to audit our books. The shell company was accidentally mentioned in an email between the stripper-banger and his friend. The accountant was curious and jumped on it, but the fine state of Delaware wouldn't tell us who the owner was. As if their *privacy* laws were more important than me getting my fair share." Her fists came up again and she pinched her face tight. "Ooh, that filthy weasel."

"Ro," Tim said, "focus."

Sure. Now he wanted her to focus. After *he* lit her up. Lucie shook her head. "When Delaware wouldn't cooperate, she got a subpoena that forced them to release the information."

"You know it, sister. We cracked that shell into a million pieces."

Subpoena. *Ooh, ooh, ooh.* Lucie shot her hand straight up and wagged it like a third grader trying to get the teacher's attention. "We should get a subpoena."

Tim set his mug on the chair's arm and stared at it with

squinty eyes. "A great idea. But we'd need a prosecutor for that. And a DA doesn't just hand those out. We'd have to give them information Mattie won't want to reveal. Such as her identity. You want to take that chance? After the press conference the Boston DA did, how do we know Mattie isn't on his list of persons of interest?"

"Ew," Lucie and Ro said.

"Yeah."

Henry chose that moment to swing the back door open. He spotted Ro and Lucie and headed straight through the kitchen to the adjoining living room. "What ew?"

Tim glanced over at him. "Hey, Unc. Good morning."

Henry eyed them all, shifting from one foot to the other. "Good morning. What ew?"

Tim took a long slug of his coffee. "We're tossing ideas around. About Mattie."

"What ideas?"

When Tim held up his mug and studied the logo on the bottom, she knew she'd lost him. *Chicken.* It always took a woman. She cleared her throat, gave Tim the stink eye, and sacrificed herself for the cause. "We need to find out who owns those four companies we found last night, but with the privacy laws in Wyoming, they won't reveal that information."

"I'm assuming you have a solution."

They sure did.

"We sure do," Tim said.

Again, she glared at him. Her man was pushing it this morning.

"Yes," Lucie said. "We have one. It's not ideal."

Henry rolled a hand for her to continue.

"A subpoena would force Wyoming to tell us the owner of the company. We could take what we've found to the

Boston prosecutor, but that more than likely means Mattie would have to be involved."

Henry cocked his head, staring at Lucie for a long moment while he pondered the idea. "You've lost your mind."

THIRTEEN

"Really?" This from Ro, whose posture went rigid as she propped both fists on her hips. "*She's* lost her mind? *Lucie*? No offense, Henry, but your girlfriend is on the lam, running from a fraud charge. She's lied to you for months and has now completely wrecked Lucie and Tim's vacation. And *Lucie* has lost her mind?"

As much as Lucie wanted to puff her chest out over her best friend's loyalty, she couldn't have her insulting Tim's uncle. "Ro," she said, "it's all right."

Ro gave her the oh-no-you-didn't lip curl. "If so, then we need to redefine what's considered all right."

"You know," Tim said. "Nutty as this is, I'm gonna agree with Ro."

"Thank you, O'Hottie."

"Hey, when you're right, you're right." He peered at his uncle. "When you think this through, you'll realize Mattie doesn't have a ton of options. And you might want to apologize to Lucie."

Holy. Moly.

Lucie shot Tim a WTH look. She couldn't blame him for

his frustration, but he needed to give his uncle—and Mattie —a break. Not everything could be fixed by law enforcement. The Rizzo family knew that all too well.

Lucie raised one hand. "Hang on."

"Damn." Tim set his mug on the coffee table. "I hate when she says that."

Hardy-har. "Listen, smarty, I have an idea. She picked up the list of developers. We have names of the four developers we think are associated with Paul Landon. Let's do this the old-fashioned way."

Ro smacked her hands together. "Yes. I like it. We'll bribe them."

Ohmygod. "No! I'm talking about *research.*"

"Research?" Ro forced a gag. "Blech. I kinda like bribery better."

Everyone's a smartass today. "No bribery." Lucie waved the list. "We're going to scour the internet for any mention of these people. Maybe we'll get lucky."

"Well, at least tell me what we're looking for."

"I have no idea. Just start searching. Anything that seems weird, screenshot it, wave a hand, yell, I don't care as long as you point it out."

Ro ripped her purse from her shoulder and added an eyeroll kicker before digging her phone out. "Some weekend getaway this turned out to be."

And there it was. Not only did Lucie and Tim's vacation get derailed, so did Ro's. It wasn't that Lucie had asked her family to help. Her loved ones didn't wait to be asked. They simply joined the mission, no questions needed.

Good people.

Dad's profession notwithstanding.

Lucie patted the spot next to her. "You're right. I'm sorry. Thank you for helping us."

"You're welcome."

"And, hey, look at it this way. The sooner we get going on the research, the sooner you'll get that walk on the beach."

The hard stare Ro hit her with should have vaporized her. *Yeesh.* Crabby.

Lucie patted the spot next to her again and Ro flopped down, swinging her hair back with a violent flick. Lucie scooted sideways, out of reach. Just in case.

"You'd better move, sister. Now let's do this. Give me a name."

They divided up the four names, each taking one. Uncle Henry disappeared into his home office to work on his desktop while Lucie, Tim and Ro made use of their phones. So much for leaving her laptop in Chicago. Her eyes might be bleeding by the time this was over.

Thirty minutes into the exercise, Ro tossed her hands in the air. "Oh. My. God. There are, like, ten thousand mentions of Anderson Bort. You couldn't give me someone who wasn't so popular?"

The fact that it had taken Ro thirty minutes to start whining was, in Lucie's mind, a genuine show of patience. Lucie would've expected it as early as five minutes in.

"Gee, Ro, I'm so sorry I didn't know the man's social status would create issues for you. Think outside the box."

"Ha! I always do. You just don't appreciate it."

"Both of you," Tim said from his spot on the armchair, "shut up."

Yikes. Ro stuck her tongue out at him. "O'Hottie is being O'Meanie today."

Lucie snorted. Couldn't help it. When Tim glared at her, she mimicked Ro and stuck her tongue out. At that, Tim smiled. Knowing him, it had something to do with a sexual fantasy and Lucie couldn't think about that right now.

She focused on Ro and her mutinous long face instead. "Narrow your search. Do Anderson Bort and Paul Landon. See if you get any hits. If not, do Anderson Bort and That Girl."

Ro put her thumbs to work, and Lucie peered down the hallway toward the bedrooms. Had Henry fallen asleep? Not a peep out of him the whole time. "Henry! Did you find anything?"

"Negative."

All righty. Onward ho.

If the Boston district attorney's office, with all their investigators, put in half the work Lucie and crew had, Paul Landon—or whoever was responsible for coming after Mattie—might be behind bars.

But, hey, far be it from her, the mob princess, to question law enforcement.

She went back to her phone and clicked on the next link referencing Fontina Capital, the company she'd assigned herself to research. A news article popped up regarding a function hosted by the Eloise Foundation that Grant Berwyn, Fontina Capital's owner, had donated fifty thousand dollars to.

Grant Berwyn.

Lucie ticked back in her mental file. She hadn't remembered seeing that name on any of the reports. She jotted down it down, just in case, but good for him supporting his community.

And it gave her another lead. She tapped Grant Berwyn into her phone. *Voila.* Twelve pages of hits. Excellent.

Or not.

Maybe Ro wasn't far off with that whining.

Lucie poked the first link. Condo building near the Boston waterfront. She skimmed the article. Three hundred upscale units overlooking the harbor. If you had at least a million bucks to spend you could call one your own. And that was only the starting price. Grant Berwyn didn't fool around.

Next link. Another charity gig. This one a Christmas gala to raise money for a battered women's shelter. Possible fraudster or not, Lucie appreciated his philanthropic endeavors.

Next. Ribbon cutting at a newly remodeled apartment building. Lucie scrolled, skimming the article and photos of smiling families. The apartments were part of a new program sponsored by the Eloise Foundation. Again with this Eloise Foundation? Berwyn had to be on the board or something. For this particular project, qualifying families were given the chance to move out of their crime-ridden neighborhoods into newly remodeled apartments in Dorchester, a diverse, family-friendly neighborhood. All subsidized by the Eloise Foundation.

In the middle of the article, a black and white photo showed a thin woman dressed in a form-fitting dress accessorized with a single string of pearls. Her short blond hair, combined with the dress and pearls, gave her that I-have-money appearance rich people perfected. Flanked by three men and three women, the photo showed her cutting a ribbon. Out of curiosity, Lucie read the caption. *Foundation director, Eloise Berwyn*—aha!—*surrounded by her husband, Grant, two daughters, April and Jess, sons, Stephen Berwyn and Simon Torrance.*

Torrance. Huh. Must be Eloise's son from a previous relationship.

Torrance, Torrance, Torrance.

"You got something?"

Lucie snapped her eyes to Tim. "What?"

"You're making that humming noise you do when you've figured something out."

Really? "I make a humming noise?"

He laughed. "Yeah. Ro, tell her."

"O'Meanie is right, Luce." She flashed a smile. "You're a hummer."

Tim let out a laugh and Lucie once again imagined his mind going straight to the gutter.

"Simon Torrance," she said.

"Boston DA." Tim shot back. "What about him?"

Lucie wasn't sure, but her jaw may have dropped. She lifted her fingers to her chin, feeling around her face. Yep. Total jaw drop.

"Luce?"

Could this be a wild coincidence? Had to be. *Ya think?* She slouched back, blew air through her lips. "This could be a coincidence."

"Doubtful," Tim said, "but go ahead."

"I'm researching Fontina Capital, owned by Grant Berwyn. Husband of Eloise. Father to April, Jess, and Stephen."

"And?"

"He has a stepson. Simon."

Tim's eyebrows hiked nearly to his hairline. "As in Simon *Torrance*?"

"You got it, detective. Fontina Capital's owner, who does business with Paul Landon and our registered agent, Helen Craft, is related to the prosecutor on Mattie's father's case."

"Oh, please," Ro said. "There is no way that's a coincidence."

Tim tossed his phone on the coffee table. "You're sure it's his stepfather?"

She pointed to the phone screen. "According to this picture."

The comment got Tim moving. He pushed off the chair and hustled back to their bedroom. He returned with the notepad he'd brought from Mattie's the night before and set it on the table in front of them before sitting next to Lucie.

On the first page was the flow chart he'd drawn connecting all the players to Helen Craft and Paul Landon. "Roll with me here." He tapped Landon's name then dragged his fingers to the developers. "He's the middleman between the developers and That Girl. Eight months ago, his son and Mattie's father were convicted on fraud charges." He met Lucie's eye. "Eight months ago. It's taken us two days to find the Helen Craft-Paul Landon-Island Investments connections. Two days, Luce."

Exactly what she'd been thinking earlier. "Begs the question, why in eight months couldn't the district attorney's office, with all their resources, find what took us two days? Or maybe they did and there's no proof?"

"Or," Ro said, "that prosecutor is a rat-bastard protecting daddy by burying evidence."

"Henry," Lucie called, the high-pitched excitement in her voice booming. "You need to hear this."

Within seconds, his head popped out of the doorway. "What is it?"

Tim waved him to the living room. "We think the Boston DA is somehow involved."

"The DA? No fooling?"

"No fooling, Unc."

Tim vacated his seat next to Lucie and sat on the arm of the sofa, so Henry could sit. She updated him on Grant Berwyn's company, the charity run by his wife and the photo with his stepson, Boston's top prosecutor.

When they were through, Henry ran his hands through his shock of white hair and let out a long sigh. "This is nuts." He looked up at Tim. "What do we do? Who do you go to when the person who's supposed to be above reproach turns out to be—"

"A rat-bastard?" Ro added. Lucie shot her a look that clearly failed to inject any fear because Ro waved her off. "You know it's true."

The doorbell rang. Who the heck was this now?

Ro held up her hand. "Allow me."

"Go ahead," Tim said, "Make yourself at home."

"Why, thank you, O'Hottie. I will. Besides, it's just Joey and the 'rents. He texted me. They're bored."

Lovely. Now they'd have to deal with Dad and Joey, too. Mom, Lucie didn't mind. Her mother might be the only sane one of the bunch.

Ro strutted to the entryway, swinging her hips as she went and drawing Henry's stare. Ah, to be a man-killer.

She stopped at the door, flipped her upper body forward to give, as she liked to say, the girls a boost before standing tall again and smoothing her clothing. Lucie smiled. No matter what, Ro always fixed herself up before Joey saw her. There was something oddly sweet in the gesture. Considering the two of them were complete maniacs who would, more than likely, wind up killing each other one day.

But love came in all different forms. Her brother and BFF seemed happy, so why not?

Ro opened the door and swung her arm in a dramatic arc. "Helloooo."

"Hey." Joey strode by Ro, smacking her on the ass as he went. "How was the walk?"

"Hands off. We didn't go."

"Joseph," Mom said, "is that nice?"

Dad, looking dapper in pressed cotton shorts and a white T-shirt, waved to the room at large. "Morning. Is coffee on?"

What was with her family making themselves comfortable in Henry's house?

"In the kitchen," Henry said. "Help yourself."

Joey waited for Mom and Ro to sit then dropped into the only open wingback chair. "What happened with the walk?"

"We got sidetracked with research," Ro said. "Turns out the Boston DA is dirty."

For crying out loud. All they needed was to get Joey and Dad on a rant about dirty politicians and cops. They'd be here for days.

Lucie gritted her teeth. "We don't know that."

"Sure we do," Ro said. "You just don't want to believe it. I love that about you."

Henry cleared his throat. "Tim, please, tell me what we should do. Can we go over the DA's head?"

"There's a couple options. We could go to the Massachusetts State Police. Their U.S. Attorney might also be a possibility. Hell, this thing involves multiple states, so the FBI might want a piece of it. Let me make some calls. I was on a task force last year with a federal agent. He might be able to help."

Before Tim could pick up his phone, Henry shook his head. "Wait. We have to ask Mattie."

Tim let out the famous O'Hottie sigh. Poor guy. Every move was put on stand-by and Tim didn't appreciate that mode.

He met Lucie's gaze, more than likely hoping she'd jump to his rescue, but...

She scrunched her nose. "Sorry, honey. I have to agree

with Henry on this one. It's Mattie's future. She should decide."

Rather than pout or kick up a fuss, Tim sat quietly, a whole lot of nothing masking his emotions. This is what she adored about him. No irritation that she sided against him, no ego trip, no pouting.

Finally, he nodded. "All right. Point taken. But let's go talk to her now, because somewhere in the next few days, I'd like to get back to my vacation."

He headed toward the door, pausing at the entryway table to grab car keys.

"Ho." Dad appeared at the kitchen doorway, mug in hand. "Where we going? I just got my coffee."

Lucie gathered their notes and followed Henry to the door. "Mattie's. You all stay here."

Before Lucie cleared the sofa, Ro vaulted from her seat. "Not a chance, sister. I lost my walk this morning to help this broad. We're not missing anything."

Tim once again shot Lucie a look. As if she could control her family? He should know better.

He held the door open. "Fine. Just...please...let us do the talking."

Good luck, fella.

Tim, Lucie, and Henry piled into the Lexus while Joey, Ro, Mom, and Dad, still carrying his coffee, decided against their rental in favor of the golf cart Ro had driven over earlier.

When this was over, Lucie had no doubt Ro would insist on cruising the streets of Franklin in an Escalade golf cart. And nobody would think twice about it. Everyone knew she was nuts. Why question it?

"Don't worry," Ro said, "We'll keep up. It has a turbo engine."

"Swear to God," Tim said, "I'm in hell."

A little dramatic for sure, but given the restraint he'd shown thus far, he deserved to spout off. Lucie climbed into the backseat and Henry started the car, letting them get buckled before moving. Safety first. Always.

After backing out of his driveway, he motored down the street, his pace far from hurried.

"What's the speed limit?" Tim asked.

"Thirty-five. I'm going thirty-four."

Oh, boy. Lucie imagined the top of his redhead blowing clear off.

Henry tapped the steering wheel. "When we get there, we should be careful about how we tell her. She's a little high-strung."

Ya think? Lucie peered out the window at the passing palm trees and bit her lip to hide the smile.

"You know her best," Tim said. "You tell her. Or at least start the conversation. You'll know what to say. Lucie and I can fill in anything you miss."

"All right."

Giving up on the palm trees and sunny morning they'd all but missed, Lucie studied Henry's profile. The sagging cheeks, the throbbing muscle in his jaw.

The misery.

He too deserved some slack. His world had been turned upside down. Lucie thought back to the day her father had been convicted of tax evasion. For years she'd lived in a swamp of denial, putting her father's lifestyle out of her mind and holding her head high. Rising above it all. At least until she saw his picture on the front page of a tabloid the day after his sentencing. Handcuffed and being led away by a bailiff, that image would stay with her forever. There was simply no way to flush it out. Worse was the headline.

JAILBIRD.

Her father's life had been summed up in one word. Eight measly letters.

Hers had been shattered that day. But this wasn't about her. This was about Henry.

On impulse, she unclipped her buckle, ignored the warning bell for belt violations, and reached between the seats, squeezing Henry's shoulder. "I'm so sorry, Henry."

"A few days ago, we were happy. Living the dream. What happened?"

"Life did," Tim said. "And you know as well as anyone life can suck."

Well, thank you, Mr. Sensitivity.

Lucie shot Tim the side-eye. Between Mattie's over-the-top personality, his mother hounding him for details, and the whole on the lam thing, she imagined he'd be conflicted. The cop in him felt the need to serve, to find the truth, but even if they proved Mattie's innocence, she knew him well enough to know he wasn't sold on her as a love match for his straight-laced uncle.

"It sure can," Henry said. "I love her, but I don't know. This is a lot."

Tim nodded. "I agree."

Here we go. She braced herself for Tim's lecture. The one that would convince his uncle to walk away. To avoid the drama this woman brought. *Dammit.* It didn't seem fair. Outside of being naive, none of this seemed to be Mattie's fault. Now she'd lose everything.

Again.

No.

She wouldn't let him convince his uncle to abandon the woman he loved.

"Tim—"

He held up his hand. "Wait. I have something to say." He angled sideways in his seat and faced his uncle. "It *is* a lot. It's your life and you sure as hell didn't sign up for this. You see what I deal with from Lucie's family."

"Hey!"

He snapped his gaze to her. "It's true. You know it is. I'm a cop in love with a mob boss's daughter. I mean, it doesn't get more twisted than that. I take heat for it every day at headquarters. It probably cost me a promotion or two."

A crushing weight forced Lucie's head to drop forward. Lost promotions. Because of her. *Ohmygod.* A spurt of tears filled her eyes. She loved this man. Adored him. And his love for her could wreck his career. "Tim, I'm—"

His green eyes were fierce and direct. "I knew going in it'd be a risk. Ask me if I care? Ask me if, for one second, I ever considered letting you go because of my job. Do it. Ask me."

She swallowed hard, fought the tears. God, she loved him. "I don't have to."

"Ask me anyway. I want my uncle to hear it."

"Did you? Ever?"

"Not once. If my superiors and co-workers want to judge us when they don't even know you, I don't need them. Fuck 'em. That's what I say."

An F-bomb. As horrible as the situation was, Lucie's chest filled, a huge burst of pride that nearly blew her ribcage apart.

Tim? Totally getting lucky when this was over.

She choked back a bout of tears, laughing at herself for coming a little unglued. Who could blame her when a man said those things? When he accepted her. Unconditionally. "Thank you," she said locking her gaze on Tim. "You have no idea what that means to me."

"No. Thank *you*. Before you my life was seriously boring. As crazy as your family is, as insane as they make me, I love them. I don't agree with half of what they do, but that's on them. It's not my issue."

For a split second, Henry took his eyes from the road, glancing at her. "His mother raised him right."

"She did," Tim said. "You're her brother. Who knows if she'll approve of Mattie, but I guarantee she'd hate you walking away before we have answers. If you love Mattie, you *stick* until you can't *stick* anymore. Don't listen to the chatter. Eventually, this'll blow over and you'll get back to living your life."

Hopefully not in witness protection.

Lucie shooed the thought away.

Eyes on the road once more, Henry nodded. Then he pushed his shoulders back, lifted his chin a la Rizzo style, and gripped the steering wheel. "Let's do this. Go time."

FOURTEEN

Lucie pumped a fist. "Yes! Good work, Henry."

Her excitement was short-lived. Half a block from Mattie's, she spotted an extra car in the driveway. "Whose car is that?"

Henry shook his head. "I don't know. Never saw it before. Maybe a new client."

If they were lucky.

Henry parked behind Mattie's car in the driveway and they hopped out. At the curb, the cart came to a screeching halt. Who knew it could go that fast?

Certainly not Dad whose coffee sloshed over his fingers and triggered a bout of yelling. His own fault for trusting Ro's driving. Still, he set the cup on the seat and wasted no time charging toward Lucie. "Who the hell taught her to drive like that?"

Up ahead, Henry opted not to use the house key Mattie had given him, knocked lightly, and waited while Joey and Ro debated her golf cart driving skills.

"I'm just saying," Joey said, "next time, I might like to not fall out."

"Now it's my fault you didn't hold on?"

Lucie whipped around. "You fell *out*? Of the *cart*?"

"She took the turn on two wheels."

"I did not."

From Mattie's porch, Tim swiveled around and gave Lucie a hard look. "Please, do something. They're killing me."

"I know. I'm sorry. Ignore them."

He snorted, mumbling something about miracles.

Whatever.

Henry banged harder. "She's not answering."

"Unc, you have a key."

"Well, yes, but she's not expecting me."

Aw, Henry. So sweet. But sweet needed a boot in the butt right now. They had things to do, crimes to solve, and he was worried about manners?

"She could be dead in there," Ro said.

Lawdy. Whirling back, Lucie gave her the stink-eye. "You're not helping."

"She's right," Dad said, "you never know."

Okay. Time to call in reinforcements. "Mom? Help me out here."

"Lois Gilbert was only sixty-one when she had a heart attack." Mom slashed her hand across her throat. "Kicked it in her sleep. That's how I want to die."

Tim rubbed two hands over his face. "And me without my gun."

In a desperate battle to not lose her mind, Lucie slammed her palms against her forehead. "I'm sorry," she said again.

How many times could she apologize to one man?

"Ma," Joey said, "don't say that. I can't think about you dying. It's not fair to make me."

"Oh, Joseph, grow up. Everyone dies."

"That's it." Henry flipped through his keyring and shoved one in. "We're going in."

Thank you, sweet baby Jesus.

Tim blew out a hard breath. "Thank you, sweet baby Jesus."

Just as Henry pushed open the door, Mattie appeared, her gaze bouncing from one person to another as she body-blocked the doorway. "Henry, hi."

"I knocked," he said. "Twice. You didn't answer."

He made a move to peer over her shoulder, but she shifted, closing the door enough to limit the view inside. "I'm sorry. Now's not a good time. You have to go."

He craned his neck, attempting to peep over her shoulder. "Go? Why?"

"It's just...not a good time."

"Who's here?"

"No one."

"There's a car in the driveway."

"Oh, that. It's Gertie's grandson. She didn't want him clogging up her driveway."

"So he clogged yours?"

"Henry, please. I'll call you in a bit. You have to go."

With that, she gently shut the door in his face. The move prompted Henry to spin on his heel, shove Tim out of the way and march from the porch. "Something's wrong. She's never done that before."

Tim followed his uncle, his long strides making up for the jump Henry got on him. "Where are you going?"

"Around the side. I have a key to that door. We're going in."

So much for him not wanting to use it.

"Good," Tim said.

Lucie, case notes in hand, followed with the Rizzo crew taking up the rear, all of them tromping over Mattie's side yard like a pack of soldiers.

"My heels," Ro said, "will be toast after this."

"I told you not to wear those dumb shoes."

As she walked, Lucie swung a fist over her head. "Don't start. *Sssshhh!*"

Miraculously, her request was met with silence. A good thing since they'd just reached Mattie's side door. A shade covered the single pane of glass, giving them zero visibility. *Dang it.* They'd have to go in blind. Something Henry didn't seem to mind one bit. He inserted his key into the lock.

"Carefully," Tim whispered.

Henry eased his hand to the right. The *snick* prompted a wince from Henry. Lucie shot Tim a look. He rolled one hand and Henry withdrew the key. Gently, he turned the knob and eased the door open.

A man's voice from the living room carried clear through the house. Something about making the right decision.

A bark sounded and Lucie couldn't help but smile. Mattie had brought her beloved dog home from the kennel. A good sign she intended on staying.

Lucie peered across the hall to the gate blocking the laundry room doorway where Mattie had penned in Aphrodite. Interesting.

Henry pointed at the gate and mouthed. "Never."

Huh. Who was here that caused Mattie to lock Aphrodite, her *pit bull*, away?

This couldn't be good.

Joey elbowed his way in front of Lucie. God forbid the man shouldn't go first in a dangerous situation. Bunch of cavemen. Every one of them.

"Listen, Natalie," the man from the living room said, "I know where your daughter is."

"You're lying. There's no way you—"

"Crawford Academy. Janelle Mournay."

"Oh, my God."

"I'll give you credit though," the man said. "It took us a little while to find her. Poor homesick kid tried to contact gramps two weeks ago. Of course, I've been watching his old account. From there, I monitored her phone. By the way, I think it's terrific you two talk so often."

"You bastard."

The man made a tsk-tsk-tsk sound. "Don't be that way, Natalie. Your choice is simple. Tell me what you know, and no one gets hurt. Cooperate and your daughter stays safe. As a bonus, I might even be able to get your father an early release date."

All righty then. This guy knew how to throw weight around.

"I don't know anything," Mattie said. "All I want is to put this behind me. I have a new life. I'm happy. I don't want anything to do with Boston. Please, leave me alone."

"I don't think you're being honest with me and, well, it's not good to lie to a prosecutor."

A prosecutor!

Tim swung back, eyes bulging. Oh, yeah, mister. From the sound of it Mattie-slash-Natalie had the Boston DA in her living room trying to, as Dad would say, shake her down.

By the time Tim turned around, Henry was on the move and heading through the kitchen. Tim caught up, latched onto his uncle's shirt and jerked him back so hard his boat shoes squeaked against the pristine tile.

Eeeek. That was loud. Concerned they'd be discovered,

everyone halted, each frozen in various positions. At any other time, Lucie would find it funny.

Ro's warm breath hit Lucie's ear as she bent low. "That squeak just screwed us."

"*Sssh!*"

"Who's there?" This from the DA. "Come out of there."

"No," Mattie cried.

From the laundry room, Aphrodite let out three rapid barks followed by the telltale banging of doggie paws against the metal gate—a sound Lucie knew all too well. Poor dog must be frantic trying to get to her mom.

Tim or no Tim, Henry elbowed his way free and charged toward the living room.

"Dammit." Tim gave chase. "Luce stay put. I mean it."

As if.

"Yeah," Joey said. "All of you, stay put."

Ro arched an eyebrow at Lucie. "Clearly, they haven't met us. Let's go."

Yeah. They stormed the hallway with Mom and Dad in tow. For a split second, Lucie considered banning her parents from the situation, but as much as she didn't want to be left out, they'd feel the same.

Besides, strength in numbers. Plus, a resident mob boss couldn't hurt.

"Let's get this guy," Ro said, pushing past Lucie and bumping her into the wall.

"Me first," Dad said.

The group of them flooded through the opening to the living room and plowed straight into the mountain known as Joey.

He turned and threw his hands up. "What'd I say?"

"Too bad," Ro shot. "We're in this together."

Simon Torrance stood twenty feet away facing Mattie

who was between him and Henry. Torrance wore a tailored suit that fit every inch of his lean body. Custom-fitted, no doubt. His short, light blond hair had enough length to be combed away from his face, accentuating the sharp angles of his cheeks and jaw.

This guy would make a great politician.

"Whoa." Simon held up his hands and peered beyond Mattie. "Who the hell are you people?"

"Friends of Mattie's," Henry said. "This is over."

"No. Not by a long shot." He gestured to Mattie. "Unless Natalie cooperates, she'll be on her way to a cell."

A muffled cry broke the silence and triggered more barking and gate-banging from Aphrodite. If that dog broke free, she'd feast on Torrance and save his carcass as a trophy.

Lucie swung to Mattie. "Don't panic." She faced Torrance again. Being Joe Rizzo's daughter had taught her the fine art of verbal swordplay. Still holding the notepad, she waved it in front of her. "We have evidence to prove your stepfather is involved in real estate fraud."

It may have been an exaggeration. A photo and a registered agent might not stack up to a prison sentence. At best, they had a few ideas. Proof? Not so much.

Simon stepped closer to Mattie, then lunged at her. *No!* He grabbed hold of her stretchy peach top and dragged her against him. Her head snapped back, and she cried out again as he yanked on her long hair.

"Oh," Ro sneered, "now *that's* dirty."

Henry lifted his fists and took one slow step closer to Mattie. "Let. Her. Go."

"Don't—" Simon jerked Mattie's head again, "—take another step."

"Please," Mattie cried, "all of you. Just...leave. This is my problem. I'll fix it. I'll hire a lawyer and you can give him the proof. We'll tell *everyone* what he's done."

Simon gave another yank, this one more vicious then the last. She yelped, then lifted her hands before thinking better of it and dropped them again. "You're evil," she said. "Now I know why no one else was ever charged."

"You think anyone will believe you? After what your father did?"

Oh, oh, *oh. Totally* unnecessary. Lucie poked her finger. "That's not *nice*." Poke, poke. Poke. "You're pissing me off."

Also pissed off, Aphrodite let out another stream of barking.

Torrance gave her a bored look. "Gee. I'm so sorry."

And then Tim was in cop mode, his big shoulders widening, filling the space with that commanding presence he'd mastered. "Everyone, settle down."

"Who *are* you people?"

"My name is Tim O'Brien. This is my uncle. He and Mattie are...friends."

Simon's gaze shot to Lucie. "You. You're the daughter."

"Another dumbass," Ro said. "Does she look *seventeen*?"

"Yeah. She kinda does."

Lucie smacked the air with the case notes. "I am *not* a teenager! Which only confirms what an idiot you are. Now let go of her or I swear I'll pummel you."

He laughed. Actually laughed. The sarcasm, the absolute condescension, fired something primitive and... violent...inside Lucie. All her life she'd been dealing with that from ignorant people who didn't take her seriously. The searing burn roared from her midsection and shot in all directions.

Done.

And then she was in motion, dropping the case notes,

letting them hit the tile with a thwack while she broke from her pack and flew at Torrance. Mattie's penciled eyebrows hiked to her hairline.

"Luce! Don't."

Sorry, O'Hottie.

Between Sonny Peppers trying to kidnap her—on the only vacation she'd had in years—and now this joker being an ass, the madness had to stop.

Had. To. Stop.

"You ruined my *fucking* vacation!"

Simon's face bunched. "Huh?"

"Ho!" Dad said. "The mouth on you. Theresa, who the hell taught her that?"

Mom gasped. "Lucia!"

Lucie's mind roared. From the laundry room Aphrodite banged on the gate again, this time adding a growl to her barking. The deep, dangerous tone erupted in Lucie's ears, making them clang. She shook her head. Forget Aphrodite. Couldn't worry about the dog now. Torrance. He needed to be dealt with.

Harshly.

Lucie leveled her gaze on him. *Get him. Make his crooked ass pay.*

As she charged, Simon swerved right, manhandling Mattie in front of him. She tripped over his foot, her curvy body giving in to momentum and tipping forward. The boobs alone could knock her off balance, but with Simon holding her, the motion propelled him forward, his body hovering over Mattie's and revealing his back.

Perfect.

Bark, bark. Bark, bark, bark.

"Aphrodite," Tim said. "Quiet!"

Lucie went airborne and—*ooff*—landed on Simon,

wrapping her legs around his waist. He let go of Mattie, shoving her to the ground, and Lucie smacked him on the head. "Hey! She's older. Be careful."

"Luce," Tim shouted. "Off!"

Nope. No can do. *Sorry, pal.* For good measure, she smacked Simon again and he swung around, attempting to buck her off.

"Get off me."

"Do you know what you've put us through?" *Smack!* "And you're supposed to be a civil servant." *Smack. Smack, smack.*

"You tell him, sister!"

Simon whipped hard to his left. *Yikes.* She may have misjudged the skinny turd's strength. She tightened her legs and hung on as he whirled. *Left, right, left, right.* Back and forth he went, nearly dislodging her on that last try. Enough. She locked one arm around his neck and—*smack*—blasted him again.

Simon gave up on the pivoting and did a full three-sixty.

More barking, then a huge crash came from the laundry room.

Uh-oh. Lucie swung her head left. Aphrodite jumped into the hallway, her nails scraping against the tile as she cut the turn and charged. Let the feasting begin.

Before Lucie got too smug, the realization hit that, yes, she was most certainly on top of Aphrodite's intended target and would therefore possibly become dog chow along with him.

"If you hurt my baby girl, you S.O.B., I'll kill you. Do you *know* who I am?" Dad made a move toward them.

Nuh, nuh, nuh, nuh. "I've got this, Dad," Lucie said. "Aphrodite! No!"

As usual, the dog ignored her and from three-feet away

leaped, her strong body slicing through the air. Lucie tightened her hold on Torrance, bracing for the—*ooff!*—impact.

Torrance readied himself, but the collision tipped him sideways. Somehow, Aphrodite bounced off him and stuck the landing, her powerful jaws snapping, which she locked around his scrawny calf and Torrance shrieked like the wuss he was.

"Joe," Mom said, her voice packed with enough energy to blow the roof off, "*don't* you dare. You're already on parole."

"Parole?" Simon said between squeals. "Who *are* you lunatics? Get this dog off me!"

"Luce!" Someone grabbed her from behind. "Off."

She snapped her head around and spotted a flash of red hair. Tim attempting to drag her off the low-life, pond scum prosecutor. Ooh, it frosted her how Torrance abused his power. And he was supposed to protect citizens? *Puh-lease.*

Rat.

Bastard.

She lifted her hand and—*whap*—smacked him again.

Joey came into view. "Aphrodite," he said in that low, stern voice that always brought the pups to heel. "Sit."

The dog paused.

"I said, sit."

Slowly, Aphrodite planted her butt.

Dammit. How did he always manage that when nothing Lucie ever did worked?

Tim's arm slid around her waist, sandwiching her between the two men. "Lucie. Get off him. Right now."

In the months they'd been dating she'd learned his vocal cues. His normal voice had a playful lilt to it. The ultra-quiet meant he'd had a long day and probably saw things on the streets of Chicago he could've lived his entire life without. That rough, gravelly edged one?

That was trouble with a capital T.

It meant her hot Irish detective was about to lose his hot Irish temper.

Bam, bam, bam. Holy moly. From the sound of it, someone put a battering ram to Mattie's front door. Aphrodite leapt into action again, barking and racing that way before Henry managed to grab her collar. "I'll put her outside," he said.

"Open up! Police!"

"Ah, Jesus Christmas," Dad said. "Just what we need."

Still behind her, Tim got right next to her ear. "This thing just escalated. Get your ass off him so I can deal with the cops."

She unlocked her legs, released her arm from Torrance's throat, and found herself sailing backward. For added drama, Torrance let out a gag, followed by a cough. As if she'd really been strangling him.

If she had, he'd know it.

Didn't stop her from kicking out and blasting him square on the butt. "You should be ashamed of yourself. Ashamed!"

"I'll have you arrested, and you'll see who's ashamed."

"Ha! Go ahead. I've been locked up before."

His mouth dropped open for a quick second, but nothing came out. Not so tough now, was he? "I have an *excellent* defense lawyer. Never mind lunch. He eats guys like you for a snack."

"She's right," Dad said. "Do yourself a favor and shut your mouth. In fact," he dragged his phone from his front pocket. "I'll call Willie now. Theresa, where's my glasses?"

"Joe," Tim said, "put that away. We don't need Willie. Yet."

Bam, bam, bam. The knock came again. "Police! Open up."

Torrance started walking, heading straight for the door. At least until Joey stepped in his path. "Dude, you think I'll actually let you open that?"

FIFTEEN

Now that Lucie had both feet on the ground, Tim shoved by Torrance, still being guarded by Joey, who was absolutely big and meaty enough to scare the hell out of any average-sized human. Plus, he had the aggressive stance and unyielding glare of a street fighter.

"Ooh." Ro sprang into action, bending low and sliding off one of her shoes. She held up the spiked heel of her sandal. "Joey, hold onto him while I carve his eye out."

Torrance's face contorted into open-mouthed horror. "Touch me and I'll have all of you arrested."

"Good," Lucie said. "We'll share a cell with you. Won't that be fun?"

Tim shook his head as he yanked on the door, revealing two officers on the porch, shoulders back, heads on a swivel as they assessed the activity.

"Good morning, officers," Tim said. "Come in."

The first cop, a middle-aged man with graying hair at his sideburns stepped inside, his eyes on Tim as he crossed the threshold. "You on the job?"

Huh. Go figure. Cops had that twisty way of recognizing

their brothers in blue. "Yeah. Tim O'Brien, Chicago PD. Down here visiting my uncle." Tim pointed at Henry. "That's him."

The younger cop, a guy in his thirties with a woefully crooked nose that had to have been broken a few times peered at Henry, then came back to Tim. "We got a noise complaint. Barking dog, people screaming, the whole bit. What's going on?"

Ha. Did he have a week?

"Officers," Torrance said, "I'm District Attorney Simon Torrance from Boston. These people are holding me against my will."

"Puh-lease," Lucie said, sarcasm dripping like gooey maple syrup.

At that, Tim flat-out laughed. "Officers, you might want to call Detective Scanlon. He's been working a case that I believe has ties to DA Torrance. Talk about prosecutorial misconduct."

"He's lying." Torrance pointed at Mattie. "This woman is a fugitive from justice. I'm down here to apprehend her."

Still holding her shoe, Ro flicked it in the air. "Keep talking. I'll take out both eyes."

Sighing, the older cop faced Tim again. "Let me guess, she's the wildcard."

"You have no idea." Tim jerked a thumb at Torrance. "But this guy? He's no slouch. Ask him if Mattie is such an important fugitive, why he's here. And not an investigator."

The older cop gestured at Torrance. "Okay. I'll bite. Why is that?"

"The case is special to me. I wanted to see her brought to justice myself."

"So you came alone?" The cop shook his head. "Sorry. Not buying it. What case does this involve with Scanlon?"

"Sonny Peppers," Tim said. "Detective Scanlon will know it."

The cop cued the radio clipped to his shoulder. "Dispatch, I need Detective Scanlon at my location. It's regarding the Sonny Peppers case."

A minute later, after confirming the detective was on his way, the cop brought his attention back to the room.

"Everyone sit down and tell us what the hell is going on. And you," he pointed at Ro. "Put that shoe on before I have to cuff you."

"Ooh," she said. "Wouldn't *that* be amusing?"

FROM HIS SPOT against the living room wall, Detective Scanlon reviewed his notes, then looked up at Tim who sat on the sofa. "What you're telling me is District Attorney Torrance here prosecuted a fraud case involving Ms. Mournay's father—"

"Berringer," Mattie said. "That's my real name."

"Sorry. Ms. *Berringer's* father and the real estate executive from That Girl."

Lucie nodded. "Correct. Ms. Berringer's father was the contracted real estate broker for That Girl. He'd locate potential buildings for new stores or for those needing to move. Both were convicted of fraud. They were in cahoots with four developers and a man named Paul Landon."

Scanlon checked his notes again. "And Landon was the real estate executive's father."

"From what we could piece together," Tim said, "it looks like he connected the developers to Mr. Berringer, who took the deal to Mr. Landon's son. Mr. Berringer would work out a deal for retail space priced higher than the market average and Landon, the son, would approve the deal on behalf of

That Girl. The developers got high rental income or sold the building at an inflated price due to the profitable leasing deal."

"The new owners inherited the lease?"

"You got it. The executive and Mattie's father would take a percentage of all the deals. That Girl executives, after spending so much on real estate, eventually figured it out. Landon and Berringer were busted."

"What about Paul Landon?"

Torrance sat taller. "My office has been unable to make a case against him."

Lucie poked her finger. "Because you haven't *tried*. It's taken us days to tie this thing together. You've had eight months."

"You're a liar."

Off came Ro's shoe. She studied the heel for a few seconds, running one finger over it and then wagging it at Torrance. "Keep it up, you. The rage I'm feeling about my weekend at the beach being ruined is only getting worse."

The older cop snorted. "You're a piece of work."

"You have no idea," Tim, Joey and Lucie all said.

"Everyone be quiet," Scanlon said. He pointed at Tim's notepad sitting on the coffee table. "Give me what you've got."

Lucie held up her hand. She wanted to bury Torrance on behalf of all unfairly judged daughters. "The summary is that we were able to tie the four developers, including a company formed by Mr. Berringer, together by the regis-tered agent on their shell companies."

"Why did Berringer form a shell?"

Mattie shook her head. "I'm not sure. He made me a partner in it, though. I trusted him, and he forged my signa-ture on the papers."

"My thought," Lucie said, "is Mr. Berringer wanted a bigger cut and intended on buying a building, renting it to That Girl and then selling it. Like all the developers, he formed a corporation in Wyoming."

"Privacy laws," Scanlon said.

"Yes. It's hard to crack a shell there."

Scanlon waved his notepad at Torrance. "And he comes in how?"

"His stepfather is Grant Berwyn, owner of Fontina Capital. One of the Wyoming companies. We haven't gotten far enough yet, but we believe the reason the elder Landon hasn't been arrested is because he can tie Mr. Torrance's stepfather to the illegal deals."

Scanlon met Torrance's eye. "You're protecting him."

"Detective," Torrance said, "you can't possibly believe this fiction."

Fiction? They'd see about that. "We have enough evidence to throw suspicion his way. Plus, we think he hired Sonny Peppers to scare Mattie."

"Why?"

"Because Mr. Torrance believes Mattie knows something, and Grant is probably afraid she'll talk. Sonny told us he picked up his payment from a building owned by Paul Landon. We think Mr. Torrance, on behalf of his stepfather, is actually the one who hired Sonny. By setting up that money drop at that building they gave themselves a layer of protection. If something happened and Sonny got caught, which he did, Paul Landon would be blamed."

"Fiction!"

"Ro, get that shoe ready."

"You know it, sister."

Tim sighed, the two cops laughed, and Scanlon banged his fist against his forehead. A typical day in Rizzoville.

Scanlon straightened up. "Here's what we'll do. Tim, Lucie, and Mattie, you're with me." He gestured to the cops. "You've got DA Torrance. Everyone is coming to the station while we sort this out."

Lucie smacked both hands against her legs. "Good." She poked a finger at Torrance. "You're going down, mister."

THAT EVENING, after hours at the police station, Mattie, Henry, Lucie, Tim, and the Rizzo crew sat around the fire pit in Mattie's yard with much-needed beverages—from wine to bourbon to Lucie's choice of lemonade. She was so exhausted that even a sniff of alcohol might drop her.

The temperature had dropped into the sixties, adding a chill to the air and giving Lucie an excuse to wrap herself in a throw she'd swiped from a giant basket in Mattie's living room.

She gazed across the snapping flames and found Mattie focused on her. "I like this blanket. I may steal it."

"Help yourself. I owe you at least that." She broke away and took in the group. "I don't know how to thank you all."

Tim swirled his bourbon and watched the reflection of the flames dance against the glass. "Don't thank us yet. We're not nearly done."

"I know, but for eight months I've been living this crazy life. Separated from my daughter, lying to Henry. It's been...hard."

Beside her, Henry clasped his hand over hers. The two exchanged a long look that Lucie hoped meant they might try to work things out.

Tim chugged the shot left in his glass. If he could have mainlined it, he probably would've. When finished, he held it up. "The good news is there's enough evidence to secure warrants and bring in a special prosecutor to sort the whole mess out. He probably had Sonny Peppers deliver that flyer about the building. Perfect way to make it look like Landon was the one who'd found you."

"That's just evil," Lucie said.

"That's only the start. I'm gonna guess Torrance has been burying evidence. At a minimum, he'll get disbarred." He faced Mattie. "The police may need your help."

"I'll give them whatever they need. I want my life back. I was terrified. Now, because of all of you, I'm free again and can bring my daughter home." She met Henry's gaze again. "I want her to see where I live now. I'd like you to meet her. If that's what you want."

For a moment, Henry stayed silent. With grown children of his own, would he even want to take on a teenager?

"I'd like that," he said.

"Blah, blah," Joey said, "can you two do this later? I mean, I don't need to know all this."

Ro let out a huff and gave him one of her hairy-eyeball death glares. "Oh, my God. Really?"

"Don't start," Lucie said. "Please. I'm absolutely begging you."

"That's it. I'm out." Dad set his empty rock glass on the side table between him and Mom. "Let's go, Theresa. There's gotta be a game on I can watch."

"Come on, Dad," Joey said. "It's early. You hungry? I could eat."

Joey always did love their father's company. Dad stood then held his hand to Mom, who grabbed hold and let him guide her from her chair.

"Sure, son."

"I'm on a diet," Ro said.

Dad laughed. "I know. Have a salad."

He wagged a finger at Lucie, Tim, Henry, and Mattie. "You four coming?"

For a second, Lucie considered it, but a glance at Henry and his wide-eyed blank stare convinced her he might need a night off from the Rizzos.

"We're good, Dad. Thank you, though." She pushed out of her chair and popped a kiss on his cheek. "Love you. See you in the morning."

A round of goodnights, handshakes, and kisses ensued before the yard went quiet again. Tim shook his head and watched Lucie's family file out. "Well, I'll say this. They know how to keep it interesting."

That they did. He leaned over, patted her leg. "We may finally get our vacation."

SIXTEEN

Three Days Later

The morning sun rose high above Islamorada, a village in the upper Florida Keys Tim had always wanted to visit. Lucie tipped her head back, soaking in the warmth of what would prove to be an eighty-degree day. The continuous roll of ocean waves brought her to a peaceful place she hadn't experienced in a long, long time.

This was what a vacation should be.

Including the man beside her. Tim reclined on his lounger, one arm hanging down, his fingers gently raking sand. Up and back, up and back, up and back. The slow movement sent Lucie's mind to last night and the naughty things they'd done on these very chairs. Nothing like a three a.m. beach romp right outside the tiny cabin they'd rented for the week.

Yowie.

Something told Lucie it wouldn't be an effort to convince Tim they should do a replay.

"Are you thinking what I am?"

She turned her head, staring straight into green eyes that made her absolutely purr. "If it's that we need to be out here at three in the morning, I definitely am."

He flashed a wicked grin. "This is why I love you."

"Because I want to have sex with you constantly?"

"There is that. But it's more knowing what you want and going for it. The way you handled the situation with my uncle didn't hurt. Most women would run screaming from that mess."

"Ha! I was just relieved it was your family instead of mine. After everything you've sacrificed to be with me, I'd never walk away. Not when your uncle was innocent in all of it. I hope they can work it out."

Another wave broke. Lucie peered across the ocean at seagulls dive-bombing, swooping down and around and back up. This is the life she wanted. Sunrises on the beach. Seagulls. Ocean waves.

And Tim.

"We'll see," he said.

What? Had that been out loud? She bit her lip, panic rising in her chest. "I'm sorry?"

He laughed. "Where did *you* just go? Henry and Mattie —Natalie—whatever the hell her name is. Isn't *that* a pisser? All of a sudden, this woman he's loved for months has a new name."

That would be the least of it. "He'll have to wrap his mind around a whole lot more than that. He seems willing though. That's a good start."

Tim lifted his hand from the sand and reached across, running his fingers down Lucie's arm. "The men in my family don't give up easily."

Didn't she know it?

"Thank goodness you boys aren't afraid of challenges."

Her phone chose that moment to blare. *O Sole Mio.* After the last few days, Lucie couldn't resist changing the ringtone.

"Lord," Tim said. "Roseanne's up early."

"I told her not to bug me unless the office was on fire."

"Luce, she called twice yesterday."

"Well, yes, but she's used to being with me all day. She was lonely. I'll get rid of her." Lucie tapped the screen. "Hi. What's up?"

"Ohmygod. Are you alone? Is O'Hottie with you?"

Lucie slanted a sideways look at Tim. "Um...yes. We *are* on vacation together. One you promised you wouldn't disturb."

"Oh, hey now, you said to call if the building was on fire."

"And is it?"

"Metaphorically, maybe."

Lucie sat up and set her feet in the sand where the morning chill hadn't quite broken yet. A cold jolt shot through her ankles. "What happened?"

"I'm sorry to do this to you."

"Ro, what is it?"

Tim swung sideways on his chair and eyed her, studying her features with that cop gaze of his. "Everything okay?"

Who knew? Lucie held up a hand. "Ro, what happened?"

"Frankie called Joey last night. I wasn't even going to tell you, but, girl, if you hear it from someone else, I'll kill myself."

Drama. Drama. But still, the lack of snark in her BFF's tone couldn't be denied. Something had rattled her. Had something happened to Frankie? She couldn't even think about it. Yes, they'd broken up. More times than she could count. And, yes, she had Tim now and wanted that future they'd talked about only days ago. But Frankie was her first love. Years, they'd been together. She never discounted that. He'd always have a piece of her and if he was sick or hurt, she'd be devastated.

She glanced at Tim. Still with the cop stare.

"Is he okay?" She asked Ro.

"Oh, he's *fine*. Just fine."

"Then what?"

"Sister hold on to your ass. He's moving back home."

Home. Lucie dropped her gaze to her lap and let out a gasp while Tim slid to the edge of his seat. "Luce? What's wrong?"

Everything.

"Luce?"

She couldn't look at him. Not now. Not when her insides were coming apart. *He's moving back home.* The words looped in her mind.

"Luce," Ro said, "you there?"

"I'm...here. Hhh...how do you know?"

"He called last night. I told you."

Right. She *had* said that.

Six months ago, Frankie announced his move to New York for a job with ESPN. He'd even asked Lucie to go with him, but they'd been broken up at the time and, well, her days of dropping everything for Frankie had ended when Tim came into her life. Still, the move, the final proof that her relationship with him was over, had rocked her emotionally.

Lucie gave up on her lap and faced Tim. Rock-solid Tim who'd never disappointed her, who'd supported her in every possible way.

He leaned in and squeezed her hand. "You okay?"

No.

She nodded. "What happened with the job?" she asked Ro.

"I don't know. I guess he'll be covering games all over the country now, so they're letting him move home."

Okay then. "Ro, thanks for letting me know."

"Of course, girlfriend. You know I love you. I couldn't let you hear it from someone else. Are you all right? You're not gonna, you know, have a freak-out are you?"

Yep. Sure am. "No. It's fine."

"You can't talk."

"Exactly."

"If you need me..."

"I know. I love you. Bye."

She hung up, let a few long seconds pass while her stomach decided whether it wanted to twist or heave. Frankie. Home. More than likely moving back into the house he still owned two blocks from her office which was just yards from Petey's luncheonette and Frankie's favorite meatball sandwich.

God. She'd have to see him.

A lot.

"Luce?"

Finally, she looked up, pasting on a way-too-enthusiastic smile. "So, that was Ro."

"I got that. What happened?"

She waved it off. "Nothing big. Turns out Frankie is moving back."

For a few seconds Tim didn't react. Just sat there with the soothing sounds of ocean waves and the morning sun glimmering off his red hair that would be strawberry blond by the end of the week.

"Interesting," he said.

So not the reaction she'd expected, but she'd roll with it. "Apparently, he called Joey last night. He'll be covering games nationwide so he's moving home."

"From a travel perspective, it makes sense. He'll be closer to the West coast."

Only Tim could be so casual about this. "Good point."

"Luce?"

"Yes?"

"You're upset."

Yes. Should she say it? Admit it and risk hurting him? After all, he loved her, brought her on an amazing vacation, and had just days ago told her he wanted a life with her. And here she was melting down over her ex-boyfriend. By now, Frankie should be a non-issue.

"I'm...surprised," she said. "That he's back so soon."

Tim shrugged. "I'm not."

"Why?"

"He's coming back for you."

Lucie shook her head. "I doubt that."

"It's true. I told you he talked to me when he was home last. That night you had the party for Ro at the office."

"I remember. But that was a while ago."

And then he did it. Instead of raging about Frankie and flying into a jealous fit, Tim moved from his chair to hers and hit her with a toe-curling lip lock that she'd think about until three a.m. rolled around again.

He pulled back, nipping at her bottom lip as he went. "Just so you know," he said, "Frankie doesn't scare me. I'm not going anywhere unless you send me packing. Whatever he wants, he's not getting it without a fight."

She'd be crazy to leave this man. Absolutely insane. She

grabbed his cheeks, kissed him hard. "I love you. You know that, right?"

"I do."

"Good. Nothing will ever change that."

The dive-bombing seagulls returned, squawking and looping overhead. Tim stared up at them for a minute, then came back to her. "Now, we're going to finally enjoy our vacation."

A NOTE TO READERS

Dear reader,

Thank you for reading *Incognito*. I hope you enjoyed the latest from Lucie and her gang. If you did, please help others find it by sharing it with friends on social media and writing a review.

Sharing the book with your friends and leaving a review helps other readers decide to take the plunge into Lucie's nutty world. I would appreciate it if you would consider taking a moment to tell your friends how much you enjoyed the story. Even a few words is a huge help. Thank you!

Want to find out what's coming next?
Sign up for my newsletter
Follow me on Facebook and Twitter

Happy reading!
Adrienne

ACKNOWLEDGMENTS

Thank you to my dear friend Cindy Palmer for helping me brainstorm ideas for Paradise City. It's always a hoot when we put our heads together.

To Tony Iacullo, thank you for walking me through the legalities of real estate fraud. Any mistakes I've made are my own, but I'm hoping I got it right. Misty Evans, thank you, thank you, thank you, for your evil plotting mind when I get stuck. Love you, sister! To my editors, Gina Bernal and Elizabeth Neal, your attention to the finer details is so appreciated! I'd be lost without your guidance.

A huge thank you to Lyndsey Lewellen for crawling inside my head and giving me another fantastic cover. Your talent astounds me. Thanks also to Amy Remus, my friend and beta reader, for taking an early peek at this book and giving feedback.

As usual, thank you to my guys who make my world a happy place. I love you.

Finally, to my awesome readers who encourage me to keep crafting stories with Lucie and her gang, I'm so grateful for your support. Muhwah!

ABOUT THE AUTHOR

Adrienne Giordano is a *USA Today* bestselling author of over twenty-five romantic suspense and mystery novels. She is a Jersey girl at heart, but now lives in the Midwest with her ultimate supporter of a husband, sports-obsessed son and Elliot, a snuggle-happy rescue. Having grown up near the ocean, Adrienne enjoys paddleboarding, a nice float in a kayak and lounging on the beach with a good book.

Don't miss a new release! Sign up for Adrienne's new release newsletter!

For more information on Adrienne, including her Internet haunts, contest updates, and details on her upcoming novels, please visit her at:
www.AdrienneGiordano.com